SWEET WATER

A Second Chance Romance

LAURIE LEWIS

Willowsport Press

SWEET WATER

A Second Chance Romance, Book 2

Laurie Lewis

To Tom
Who still leads me to sweet water.

CHAPTER ONE

The fog of medication lifted enough for Olivia McAllister to flutter one eye open and see the cold frame of bars surrounding her elevated bed and the chaotic network of wires and tubes snaking across her barely gowned body; all confirming that her nightmare was true. There had been an accident. A terrible accident.

An athletically built woman with long brown hair stood by the window. Her angular jawline and strong brow, Jeff's signature features, identified her as her sister-in-law Susan. The two women had only met once, some eleven years ago, when Jeff brought his baby sister to the University of Washington's Seattle campus to celebrate her high school graduation. The pride she displayed while being escorted on her football-star brother's arm was now replaced with grief, dispelling any hope Olivia had about the outcome of the accident.

Jeff was gone.

Olivia lowered her eyelids, shutting out the conscious

world again even as the soft whoosh of the door brought in light from the noisy hall and someone else into the room. After introducing herself to Susan, the physician moved to Olivia, brushing the tangled mass of dark hair away from her bandaged shoulder.

"Mrs. McAllister. Mrs. McAllister ...? Please open your eyes for me, Olivia."

When Olivia didn't respond, the physician's citrus scent moved closer. She forced each of Olivia's eyes open and passed a light back and forth across them. Olivia's mind surrendered to the medication again, grasping hold of a recent memory as it retreated.

A picnic. With oranges.

Flashes, like lightning strikes, followed. A checkered table-cloth. A bag of orange slices. Happy faces. A kind woman. A small child. Laughing men tossing a football. The football wilted in midair as she watched herself and Jeff enter their extravagant Lexus sedan to drive away. An icy spray of fear dismissed the images as the doctor called her name again.

Olivia's mind ignored the summons to consciousness as the images of that picnic taunted her peace. She heard another veiled call from the doctor, who tapped on her inner arm above the IV, but Olivia felt no compulsion to open her eyes and respond. Silent moments passed until the quiet was broken by a question on the topic Olivia most wanted to forget.

"Do you know what caused the accident?" the doctor asked Susan. "I hear they were both out of the car."

"I only know what the police told me," said Susan. "That a truck was taking the turn on a mountain road when my brother was crossing four lanes of traffic on foot. The driver swerved, but—" Her voice caught, and then she continued. "He clipped the car, which was parked on the narrow shoulder. They think that's where Olivia was standing. She was thrown about twenty feet." Susan's voice broke, and she paused before continuing. "None of it makes any sense."

The discussion ended, and the door eventually swished closed, darkening the room once more. Olivia's mind rewound to the drive from the picnic, which replayed in a staccato pattern of still photos, each one popping up like tissues being torn from a box. The replay paused on a face filled with anger. Jeff's face. For a moment, Olivia wondered at the reason for his anger, and then she remembered his reaction to the news she'd shared. Happy news that led to tragedy.

She longed for someone to hold her, to make everything all right. A face came to her. Not Jeff's face, but that of another man. The sweet warmth it brought quickly soured, leaving her utterly alone. Voiceless moments passed, interrupted only by the sterile beep of monitors and the faint street sounds below. And then the door opened again.

Olivia heard a cry break from Susan, followed by rapid footsteps and muffled weeping. "You came. Thank you."

"I'm so sorry, Susan."

Olivia tensed. The male voice was familiar, yet strange. Eight years had matured it, deepened it. Eight years and unimaginable wealth had added an air of poise and confidence the owner had lacked in his youth. He had once been her best friend, her confidant, but not now. Now he was her enemy. The man responsible for destroying her family.

She heard Susan choke out, "I'm sorry for bothering you. My parents are devastated. You were the only other person I could think to call."

3

His voice was raspy as he replied, "Of course I'd come."

The full gamut of emotions, pent up over a twelve-year roller coaster of struggles, roiled in Olivia's battered body, pushing past the medicated fog. "Get out," she muttered weakly.

Susan rushed to her. "You're awake! Hudson, catch the doctor. Tell her—"

"Get out," Olivia repeated more audibly, clenching her jaw so tightly she shook as she turned her head toward the man. She forced her eyes to open long enough to meet his. "Get out. You're not welcome here. Get out! Get out!"

HUDSON BAUER HAD DINED with royals, danced with starlets, and negotiated with business titans across the globe, but none of those experiences had been as daunting as entering Olivia's hospital room. He caught only a quick, disconcerting glance at her when he entered before moving into Susan's waiting arms. That one stolen glimpse of Liv, bruised and swollen, her wounds wrapped in gauze or splinted, was enough to reopen the gash in his heart, and then he froze as she splayed him open.

He had prepared himself for the emotional tsunami seeing her would launch, but he was not prepared for her rage. Their eyes connected, and for a second, they were back in time: a geeky computer science major and the shy, leggy coed he first saw in the library at the University of Washington. And then it was gone, replaced by anger and something else.

The look in her eyes froze him where he stood, making him an inanimate target for her fury. He racked his brain to recall eyes that had affected him similarly, and then he knew. He had been in Rashaya, Lebanon, a day ago, setting up funding for humanitarian groups handling the flood of Syrian refugees flowing into that country. Those refugees bore the same look he now saw in Olivia's eyes. Not the hollowness of hunger, but the vacant look of defeat.

For a second, he regretted coming, but ignoring Susan's message about the accident had never been an option. That he received it at all was a miracle. He had completed the tour of a refugee camp when the text arrived from Alejandra, his personal assistant, telling him about a curious call—Susan's— made to a corporate number she had found from a Google search of his name. The switchboard operator had inadvertently put it through to his personal line. He was on a plane within an hour, flying halfway around the world to see a woman who had left him broken and empty.

In a moment, Susan was beside him, urging him into the hall. She kicked the door closed with her foot and said, "Hudson, she doesn't know what she's saying."

"No. She knew exactly who I was. She meant every word." He ran his hands through his tangle of brown curls. "I was prepared to find her grieving, but she blames me. For what? For this? What has Jeff told her these eight years?"

Susan's shoulders slumped. "I'm sure you have a pretty good idea."

She leaned against the wall, her head flopping back as if her neck couldn't bear its weight. "I should be sad and grieving. I've lost my only sibling. Instead, I'm just so angry. I've hardly heard from Jeff in eight years, and now I'm expected to handle this?" She groaned and dropped her head into her hands. "I'm sorry. I don't really mean that."

Hudson moved beside her.

"I really did love my brother. And I think Olivia and I could have been friends under other circumstances."

"Could have been? You blame Liv?"

"Jeff was always Jeff—an irresponsible, party-loving jock with a flock of gorgeous dates. Olivia had to know that. From what I see, she's the one who changed."

It was true. Hudson regretted introducing the awkward University of Washington coed to Jeff almost immediately. Jeff had no interest in Liv beyond what tutoring help she could give him, but Hudson clearly remembered how quickly she morphed from a geeky scholar who was more comfortable writing HTML code than love letters to a shy beauty soon after he inserted her into the odd friendship he enjoyed with his high school jock friend, Jeff. He felt like a harness over the next four years, stabilizing two very different members of the trio while maintaining a healthy separation between Liv and Jeff. He told himself it was for the good of the work, but he knew it was more. Even though the pair showed an outward indifference to one another, Hudson knew Liv turned herself inside out to impress Jeff.

He raised his hand, ending further excavation of their buried pasts. "I don't suppose who did what to whom matters anymore."

"It evidently does to Olivia."

Desperate to segue on to a different topic, Hudson asked about Olivia's health. "What are the doctors saying?"

Susan gathered her hair and twisted it nervously. "She was thrown down a ravine when the truck hit the car. Something cut her leg pretty badly. They say she lost a lot of blood. Other than scrapes and cuts, her worst injuries are soft tissue damage to her shoulders and knees." Susan's hands dropped to her sides. "Except... she lost her baby, Hudson. I don't even know if Jeff knew he was going to be a father."

Hudson's heart stuttered and his palms went clammy. He rubbed them against the front of his jeans as he slid down the wall into a squat to break eye contact and hide his reaction to Susan's ongoing report.

"They're running more tests, but she's going to need a good deal of rehab. They want her to stay close by if possible, but I don't know what to do. My parents moved out of state, and my place is two hours away. Plus, I need to be back at school by mid-August to train on new equipment."

Her shoulders slumped in defeat. "I'm sorry, this shouldn't be about me. It's just that an anonymous donor completely funded a new, fully equipped school specially designed for disabled students. It's everything I've fought for, but what do I do about Olivia? I've been through her wallet, and I can't find any contact information for her mother or even a physical address or an insurance card for her, so I told the doctors I'd make local arrangements for her convalescence."

Hudson released a rush of breath and stood again. He pulled his key ring from his pocket, removed two keys, and pressed them into Susan's hand. "I bought my parents' Cannon Beach house. Here are the spare keys to the front door and the key to the Nissan in the garage. You and Olivia can stay there and use the car for as long as you need."

Susan's eyes glistened as her hand closed around the keys. "Thank you," she muttered, bringing her hand and the keys to her breast. "I know your parents' place was the closest thing Olivia had to a home during your college years."

His heart clenched over the comment. He quickly changed the subject. "How are your parents?"

Her lips trembled. "Not good at all. Jeff never introduced Olivia to them, and the only contact we've had with him was a few calls over the years. He closed a door on all of us. But the news was still devastating. He was their only son."

An awkward silence passed between them until Susan asked, "How are your folks? Jeff only took me to one of your working luaus, but I loved that weekend and your parents."

Hudson smiled. "They're great. They're in Africa, working on a water project for the WHO."

"The World Health Organization? So now your folks are helping you save the world?"

"Villages need water. Dad always was the best well driller in Tillamook County. I just made the introductions."

Another awkward pause ensued while Susan stared blankly at the floor.

"I know you're overwhelmed right now. Liv was never close to her mother. She never wanted to talk about their relationship, so there might not be much help there, but we can hire help once she's released. And don't worry about school. We'll make sure you meet all your deadlines."

"Thanks, Hudson. I really am excited to start this new year. I'd love to thank the donor who made this possible."

"I'm sure they'd tell you their part was easy compared to what you do every day."

She squeezed the keys again. "And thank you for these. Olivia can recuperate where she'll feel comfortable."

Hudson reached into the breast pocket of his white button-front shirt, withdrew two cards, and handed them to Susan. "Here is my personal business card. You can always reach me at that number. And I stopped by the bank and arranged for this preloaded bank card for any expenses that come up ... at least until Liv can sort things out."

Susan touched the gold-embossed "HB" with her finger. "This is the very card I would have expected from you. Elegant, unpretentious. Hudson Bauer ..." Her hand swept through the air as if she were drawing a marquee. "You're an icon, like The Boss or Madonna."

"Now you're making fun of me," he teased.

"You've probably placed this card in the hands of famous people I only read about ... but I'm glad you're still a regular guy."

"Money doesn't make one person better than another. It's just a tool." Then he tapped the card. "The only thing that matters right now is that it allows me to get here in a few hours no matter where I am." Despite his wealth, a sense of powerlessness slammed Hudson, rounding his shoulders. "I wish I could do more. I planned to stay right there in her room and relieve you, but ..." He looked at Olivia's door and shook his head. "I'm the last person she wants to see. Just promise to call me if you or she need anything. I mean it."

"I promise."

CHAPTER TWO

A hospital chaplain arrived during Olivia's rant, but when his efforts to comfort her failed, sedation was ordered. She welcomed the fog until her last fateful drive and conversation with Jeff began replaying in a subconscious loop. As the effects of the medicine decreased, the clarity of the memory increased until she was there beside the car again, watching Jeff walk away. But this time, she knew what would happen next. Her mumbled warning for Jeff to come back went unheeded, and her panic increased until she bolted upright, yelling, "Watch out! Watch out!"

Monitor leads and her IV hose whipped loose despite Susan's efforts to still Olivia's flailing arms. The beeping alerts sent nurses scrambling while Susan was relegated back to the reclining chair she had slept in the past few nights. Olivia noticed the stress on her sister-in-law's face. The quiet teacher had questions she needed to ask, questions that denied her peace, and the time had come for them to talk.

After the nurses left, Olivia closed her eyes and brushed her long, dark hair away from her face with her least encumbered hand before resting the arm across her brow. Opening her eyes, she met Susan's gaze. "I haven't thanked you for staying with me. We haven't really spoken since—"

"Since your secret wedding eight years ago?"

There it is. Olivia stiffened at Susan's quiet but well-aimed reproach that revealed her own pain.

"Do you know how my parents found out that their only son had brought a new member into the family? Facebook. Some of Jeff's football buddies posted photos."

How could they have been there? We had only been engaged for an hour.

There had been no thought of parents. No thought of anything, really. Now, it was clear the McAllisters blamed her for the family's estrangement. "I'm sorry. It all happened so quickly. We ... just didn't think."

"No, you didn't," Susan muttered, dipping her head, clearly uncomfortable over causing Olivia pain.

"How did you hear ... about the accident?"

Susan fumbled with her hands. "Jeff called unexpectedly yesterday morning. He said he was returning to Portland for a week or so and wanted to get together. I was so excited..." She bit her upper lip and wiped her eyes. "Anyway, the police saw my number on his phone and called me since there was no emergency contact info for either of you and only a series of P.O. boxes for an address."

Olivia cringed as she heard how irresponsible they sounded. "I'm sorry. Thank you for everything you've done for me." Unable to hold the tears back any longer, she wept into her blanket. Susan looked aside until she regained control.

"Would you help me … Would you help me plan his service?" Olivia's voice caught.

The topic seemed to suck the air from the room. The awkward silence that filled the void was finally dispelled when Susan coughed to clear the emotion from her own voice. "My folks arrived last night. They would appreciate being included in those plans."

Olivia swallowed and nodded. "Of course."

Another long, silent pause magnified the tension in the room until Susan spoke. "This was the first time Jeff's been home in years, and he didn't keep in touch with anyone from here as far as I know, so it'll be a small service. Just us and a few old family friends."

Olivia thought of the family with the oranges and the red-haired toddler, but she couldn't recall their names.

Susan sniffed. "He had a hymn he sang and played on his guitar as a kid." She bit her lip again and turned away.

Olivia had forgotten that he sang and played guitar. The only time she could remember such a moment was when he entertained a date during a summer campfire on the beach. Never to her. She wished she had known that he had attended church. She'd been married to the man for eight years and knew as little about him as he knew about her. The depth of their marital failure slammed her. "Let's use the one you remember, if you think it would please your parents."

Susan nodded. Her hands twisted nervously, and then she looked up. "Did you love him?"

Olivia swallowed hard, and Susan pursued the question.

"I-I'm sorry. I'm trying to understand why he cut us out. I'd prefer to imagine him happy and self-absorbed over miserable and ashamed to come home. Why did you marry so quickly and stay away? Did you love him?"

Olivia didn't want to answer, but neither did she want to lie. "I-I-I thought so." She could hear how hollow the words were. "I tried to love him, but he didn't seem to want to be loved by me." Olivia's slim, olive-toned fingers toyed with the edge of her bedsheet. "He didn't seem to like himself much either."

"My proud, arrogant brother? That doesn't sound like Jeff at all."

Every word was being weighed, and the strength of Susan's rebuttal caused Olivia to shrink back into the mattress. "He changed after the wedding. We had just graduated, and he and Hudson were launching a promising software company. Jeff could have had his pick of women, but he pursued me, a girl with no dating experience. He said he loved me, but I suppose he woke up that first morning and realized the mistake he had made."

Susan slumped, mirroring Olivia's defeated posture. Her voice was softer when she asked, "Then why not call it a mistake, go your separate ways, and be happy?"

This was the precipice upon which Olivia had spent the last eight years, with each day hanging just a word or a look away from the fall into a marital separation. Walking that narrow line had worn her down, but failure and abandonment seemed equally terrifying to the young woman she once was, an insecure youth who voiced her surly opinion about her beautiful mother's miserable but convenient marriage. So Olivia had stayed, but why had Jeff?

She closed her eyes against the sting and shifted in the bed, wanting to close that chapter in her thin book of memories. But Susan was still staring at her, waiting for an answer, so Olivia supplied the only one she had. The only one that made any sense to her.

"The day after our wedding, Jeff drove us back to the apartment he shared with Hudson. It had also been the headquarters for our software company, but Hudson had vacated the place. All he left was an envelope with a note for Jeff, berating him for missing their big presentation and describing how he'd stumbled through it alone and closed the deal."

"Did he know why Jeff missed the presentation? That you two had eloped?"

Olivia shrugged. "Evidently. I was so stunned that I never actually read the letter, but Jeff told me what was in it. He read a line to me that said, 'I hope you're happy.'"

"Maybe he meant it. Maybe Hudson was actually wishing you guys well, and he moved out to give you two some privacy."

Those had been her first thoughts too, but all the other evidence was stacked against Hudson. "I admit that Jeff and I got ourselves off to a rocky start. Shutting you and your parents out was wrong, but Hudson left us nothing to build on when he stole the partnership away from Jeff."

"Partnership?"

"Hudson designed a software program that evaluated players' stats and predicted what strategies would work best against different opponents. He set up an LLC, and I wrote the programming. Several NCAA teams were interested."

"And he made Jeff a legal partner?"

Olivia shrugged again. "I suppose it was more of an understanding Jeff said they had, but even though the concept was Hudson's, Jeff was the face of the company. He knew the sports lingo, and he could talk to anyone, especially the crowd looking at that program. But Hudson reneged on everything and kept the company. One success led to another for him, but he destroyed Jeff that day."

"So that's why you lashed out at him." She shifted in her seat. "I guess I still don't understand why you and Jeff chose to stay together and be miserable."

The question wouldn't go away. Olivia surrendered to her fatigue, allowing her eyes to drift closed, ending the interrogation but not the mental examination of the question. Why did she stay? She knew. Once the shock of Hudson's departure sank in, Jeff kicked the desk, cursed, and paced in a circle. Panicked, he turned to Olivia.

"You wrote that code. I wrote the sales pitch. We're two-thirds of the dream team. We'll just start again ... make our own company." The light returned to his eyes as he extended his hand to her. "Deal?"

The proffered partnership wasn't the bond of two lovers, but it fit a pattern with which she was familiar. Jilted by Olivia's father while pregnant, her beautiful mother dated many men, keeping her eyes peeled for a suitable opportunity. When she found Louisiana plumbing contractor Peter Thibodeaux, a quiet Cajun man with a profitable business, she packed up her daughter and their things and headed to the altar.

As a child, Olivia was almost glad she wasn't pretty. Gangly and nearsighted, with a narrow, aquiline nose, long black hair, and an olive complexion like the Greek father she never met, she didn't share her mother's need to fend off suitors. Education became Olivia's ticket to stability, and she threw herself into her studies, joined the nerd clubs—

computer science and math—and applied for every scholarship she could find. Then she accepted the offer from the school farthest from her mother—the University of Washington in Seattle.

The library became her refuge. That was where she clicked with another freshman math nerd—Hudson Bauer—the high school buddy and personal stat-man to Jeff, the freshman Adonis at tight end. Hudson introduced her to Jeff, and their odd threesome worked somehow.

But it was Hudson she gravitated to. They were never at a loss for conversation. There was always a question to solve or an idea to puzzle over together. They rolled their eyes as Jeff's conveyer belt of fantasy dates strolled past while Hudson envisioned a way to turn the game strategies he provided Jeff into a marketable program.

He offered Olivia a crucial role. For the first time, she felt she belonged somewhere, that she was needed, and her confidence soared. But all the while, Olivia secretly wished Hudson would close the laptop and look at her the way Jeff looked at his dates.

With that in mind, she adopted some of the styles and trends of the girls Jeff dated. She cut and highlighted her hair, got contacts, tried makeup, and bought stylish clothes. Jeff applauded the changes that left Hudson wary and unsettled. As disappointed as she was over his lukewarm response, she liked the confident woman looking back at her from the mirror.

The next three years of building the company were the happiest of her life. Until the night Jeff swept her off her feet. And Hudson went away. Until she realized that the confident woman in the mirror had surrendered to the insecurities of her youth, and the love-filled marriage she dreamed of had become a business with occasional benefits.

Why did she marry Jeff? She told herself it was infatuation, but deep down she knew there was something else, something far less romantic. Why did he marry her? It was the question she had feared to ask him, and now that he was gone, she'd never know the answer.

CHAPTER THREE

The scent of pine filled Hudson's nose as he drove his silver Range Rover north along the Pacific Coast Scenic Byway. He passed alternating stands of straight, soaring evergreens and swatches of bare land cleared by logging, now dotted with new plantings for the future. His stress eased as the familiar sights and smells overtook him.

He pulled off U.S. Highway 101 and cruised the downtown area of quaint Cannon Beach, Oregon, popping in at the Family Market. After picking up some carefully selected groceries and supplies, he headed for the Bauers' gray, cedar shake-sided home on Forest Lawn Drive.

He could almost feel his parents' absence. The home seemed to miss them too. Ocean breezes blew trash into the shrubs, and lichen had crept across the gray cedar shake roof, leaving yellow-green patches.

His cares eased as he carried the groceries around to the back of the house to take in the spectacular ocean view. He had travelled the world to places most people only dream of, but this lot, selected by his great-grandfather, a Blackfoot Indian and logger, was his favorite spot on earth.

The powerful, never-ending expanse of churning blue met an almost equally blue horizon. Gulls squawked, waves crashed, and children squealed from the beach below the bluff where the old gray house stood. Hudson looked left to the massive, famous Haystack Rock of Goonies fame and to the sea garden that stretched from the beach to the rock and its caves. The scene was filled with memories. His favorites included Liv.

He stepped onto the sprawling porch, unlocked the French doors, and disarmed the alarm. A tautness surrounded his heart since seeing Liv. He felt it release as he stepped into the timeless house—a time capsule fitted with familiar, comfy furniture in blues and corals. The white walls and gray wood floors of the open dining/living space flowed into the kitchen. Long-stifled images returned of Liv eating at the counter or lounging on the sofa in an oversized T-shirt and jeans. Feeling wrung out, he slumped onto a stool and imagined her here again—hurt, injured, afraid. How had they gotten to this agonizing point?

He stood and began emptying the grocery bags. If Liv wouldn't see him, he'd at least make sure the old place was ready in case she accepted his offer to recuperate here.

His phone buzzed distinctively in his pocket. It was the ring reserved for Alejandra, his assistant. He took the call and waited expectantly for her Latin inflections.

"I'm trying very hard not to bother you."

"It's okay. What's up?"

"Have you even seen the news? There was another

terrorist blast near Rashaya."

The hairs on his arms stood on end. "Were any of our people hurt?"

"No, but some of the investors are pulling out. They think it's too risky to move forward at this time. HSB agrees. What do you want me to do?"

Hudson ran a hand over his face and sighed. HSB was the Humanitarian Services Branch of TBG, The Bauer Group, his sprawling corporate umbrella that now required teams of people to manage. Rashaya was the Lebanese city where he was trying to launch family-based microbusinesses to help the Syrian refugees.

Alejandra cleared her throat. "Shall I transfer corporate funds to cover the losses?"

"Not yet. Money isn't the problem. We need to get more people invested in the project … people who will care enough to mentor these new business owners. Call the AMAR Foundation. Tell them we have the capital if they have some volunteers. Get back to me when you hear from them. And double the number of security people there, no matter what it costs."

"Will do. I do have some good news. Arthur Baswell of Micro-Gear has a prototype of that solar pump to show you."

"That's great. Set up a video chat. I want to see that ASAP."

"I'll get on it. This is a delicate time for you to go dark on me. Whatever has taken you away must be pretty important."

"I'll do better about checking in."

He wasn't ready to tell Alejandra why he excused himself from critical meetings, shifted responsibilities to others, and walked away from his corporate world with only an hour's notice. It wasn't like him. Except where Liv was concerned.

CHAPTER FOUR

A ides arrived almost hourly, delivering packages containing expensive brands of personal items lost in the accident. A large bouquet of yellow tulips arrived, along with several novels and a teal-colored robe. Olivia assumed the items had been purchased by Hudson or one of his people, and while Olivia received the needed goods with initial discomfort, it did not go unnoticed that he had remembered her favorite flowers, author, and color.

Susan began staying at a local hotel with her parents after she and Olivia talked. Her parents arrived at the hospital with her one afternoon, carrying a bag that contained a new dress and shoes for Olivia to wear to the upcoming funeral. She couldn't imagine what that agonizing errand had cost them emotionally, and though their kindness was genuine, a suffo-cating curtain of guilt and blame shrouded all of them each time the conversation drifted to Jeff. She wept when they left, wondering why Jeff hadn't taken her home to meet his parents. She could only assume it was because he hadn't wanted them to meet her.

A soft knock sounded on the door before it opened slightly, revealing a woman with short brown hair and a kind face. She held a Mason jar filled with day lilies and orange poppies.

"Hello," the woman said. "Is it all right if I come in?"

Olivia wiped her eyes and nodded.

"I've been calling Susan every day to check on you." Her smile quivered. "I'm so very sorry about Jeff. We'd like to help if there's anything … anything at all you need."

Olivia muttered "thank you" to the nameless woman.

"Ben and I left the park as soon as we got the car packed and Joey cleaned up. We must have arrived just a few minutes after the accident."

The harrowing words caused Olivia to slump into her bed. "We've met before?"

The woman set her flowers down and stepped back. Two fingers covered her mouth as apologies rambled out. "I'm so sorry. We only met that day. I shouldn't have assumed—"

"Wait," said Olivia, as the fog cleared and fragments of that last day shifted into place. She remembered the checkered tablecloth spread across a picnic table under a towering tree. And a small boy digging in the nearby sand. She saw Jeff and a man tossing a football through a gap between two branches, and … "You had sliced oranges."

The woman laughed nervously. "Yes. Orange slices are the only thing I can get Joey to eat besides bread and cheese sticks."

"You're married to Jeff's high school friend."

The woman's smile returned. "Yes. Ben Ashburn is my

husband. I'm Laurel."

"You found us after the accident?"

She nodded slowly. "Jeff left his wallet on the picnic table when you drove off. We tried calling you, but no one answered. Then Ben remembered Jeff saying his next stop was the Charter Bank in Hillsboro, so we headed that way. We had only gone a few miles when we saw the flashing lights."

Olivia remembered Jeff ignoring a call. Why? Because they were fighting. For the first time that she could remember, Olivia had challenged Jeff. But why this time? She bit her lip as her hand fell over her barren belly. She had done it for the baby she would never know.

"I shouldn't have come so soon. Instead of helping, I'm adding to your distress. I just wanted to return this, and to let you know I'm nearby if I can do anything for you. Again, I'm so very sorry for your loss." Laurel laid Jeff's wallet on the bed table and stepped back.

"No. Please. Don't go," said Olivia, as she tore her eyes from the wallet and pulled herself together. "You're helping me remember. Tell me about that day. Please, sit."

Laurel Ashburn was tentative as she sat on the edge of the recliner. "That picnic meant the world to Ben. To both of us. Hudson comes back from time to time, but no one had heard from Jeff in years, and then we read what he posted on the reunion site and realized Beaverton had two successful sons that put us on the map. Well, the thought that such successful people would make personal time for an old high school friend made Ben feel very special."

Such successful people ... Olivia cringed inwardly and stretched a hand out toward Laurel. "I'm the one who envies you and your wonderful life. You have each other, a successful business, roots in a town you love, and you have your beautiful son."

Laurel touched a blush-warmed cheek. "Thank you. That's kind of you to say. Our life is simple, but it suits us. I read Jeff's reunion post. I can't imagine a life like yours, racing coast to coast between big advertising offices. But Ben appreciated Jeff's interest in his little dream. He loves building, and he's good at it. He hopes to move along with the plans he and Jeff made."

An uncomfortable chill snaked up Olivia's spine. "Remind me about Ben's plans."

"His father owns a thousand acres of timberland near the county line. If they hire a company to come in and clear-cut it, they'll only get a fraction of the value of the lumber, but hiring a crew and leasing equipment would cost them a fortune they don't have, so they gave up on the dream of developing that land until Jeff offered to help."

Prickles appeared on Olivia's arms. Their only shame to this point was self-aggrandizement. Jeff theorized that more territory meant more opportunities, so they set up a premier website for a company called McAllister and McAllister Marketing, or MMM, and bought post office boxes in New York, Tampa, Dallas, and L.A. to establish a presence in each of those lucrative markets.

Despite their tireless work, MMM failed to land any clients bigger than the small businesses who advertised in the coupon booklets and mailers they distributed. It was a legitimate enterprise that made a decent profit, but the four-market strategy required them to be mobile, living in short-term, pre-furnished rentals while everything they owned was stuffed in their car. Jeff promised Olivia they would settle down where and when he landed one big client or the right connection that would launch their company. Olivia feared he was counting on Ben to be that opportunity. But what was he planning to use as capital?

"Do you remember the terms of Jeff's offer?"

Laurel jumped to her feet. "I-I didn't come here asking you to fulfill it."

"I understand. Please … You're helping me put the pieces of that last day back together."

Laurel returned to the chair and sat stiffly. "There's not much to tell. Our high school reunion committee put that Facebook group together to gather info on the class. Ben posted about his logging and development dream. A few days later, Jeff called to say he'd seen Ben's post, and he'd like to discuss the development project. He said he was coming to Portland in a month, so we arranged that picnic. While the guys were tossing that football around, Jeff told Ben he was going to see his banker in Hillsboro to set up a line of credit while Ben got bids on leasing the logging equipment."

Olivia's hands wrung as she weighed Laurel's words. How was he planning to get a line of credit? Olivia closed her eyes to think. She handled the family/corporate finances, which amounted to less than a thousand dollars she'd managed to protect from Jeff's other pie-in-the-sky investments. In fact, they were fighting over finances in the car the day of the accident. That's why she chose that minute to tell him about the baby.

Rather than discuss things rationally, Jeff stopped the car, told her he couldn't do "this" anymore, and then blindly walked into the road and into the path of an oncoming truck barreling around the bend. She shivered at the memory.

Their financial fallout was now expanding. What was Jeff thinking when he contacted Ben Ashburn? But Jeff wasn't the only one with poor intentions. How could she have ever thought that hiring an internet attorney to go after Hudson was an acceptable strategy?

Olivia raised her head and looked at Laurel. "Laurel, the truth is, McAllister and McAllister is in the red. We're broke. As badly as Jeff may have wanted to help Ben, we couldn't get a line of credit right now. So please tell Ben not to take a risk based on anything Jeff offered."

Laurel nodded and smiled. "I kind of felt that something wasn't quite right. That there was a strain between you. Money troubles can do that to a couple, even when both people love each other." She walked over and placed a hand on Olivia's arm. "Maybe we're not so different after all. I'd like to stay in touch if that's all right. Maybe you could use an extra friend while you're here."

Mixed-purpose tears stung Olivia's eyes. She was free from her suffocating secret, and she had a new friend, but there were new questions and loose threads she'd have to deal with. Like the lawsuit she had filed against Hudson.

Susan returned alone and stood in the doorway, listening to the conversation. "Susan ... this is—" Olivia's mind went blank.

Laurel turned and offered Susan her hand. "Hi. We finally meet in person. I'm Laurel Ashburn."

"So nice to put a face with the name." Susan turned to Olivia. "You've got a good friend here. She checked on you every day."

Laurel smiled at Olivia but addressed her remarks to Susan. "I meant what I said on the phone. I'm here if I can help. You've got my number. Seriously … call me." With a final smile at Olivia, she was gone.

Olivia held her breath, waiting to see if Susan would mention the conversation she had overheard. "I didn't know you were coming back today. Is everything all right?"

She pulled a newspaper from her purse and handed it to Olivia. "We saw this in the gift shop. Reporters tied you and Jeff to Hudson. They're digging into every aspect of your lives and making my brother look like some jealous fraud who scammed people while chasing classmate Hudson Bauer's success."

Olivia sat up and faced Susan. "Our company was real. An LLC. We went to work every day. In fact, work was nearly all we ever did until our marriage was little more than a continuous business meeting. Jeff may have pretended he was already what he hoped to become, but he found clients and accounts in all those cities, and I made sure that every contract was fulfilled and every debt was paid."

"Thanks for telling me that. My parents adored Jeff. These stories describe a man they don't recognize at all. Reading them was like losing him again." Her head tilted to the side. "It was easy to blame you for Jeff's withdrawal from the family, but I overheard your conversation. I'm willing to admit that we may have gotten that wrong."

Susan blew her nose and sighed. "We ran into one of the interns on your case. You will be discharged tomorrow morning. We can proceed with the plan to hold Jeff's memorial service in the afternoon."

Tears welled in Olivia's eyes.

"And there's something else. I'm sorry, Olivia, but my parents need me." Her voice broke and she quickly recovered.

"I'm all they've got now, and I have so little time before I report back to school. I need to spend it with them."

Olivia nodded, fully aware that the fear she felt inside was apparent on her face.

"I know this sounds harsh, but for the first time, I'm trying to be a good sister-in-law to you, so listen to me. I'm willing to give you the benefit of the doubt on the past, but that means what happens going forward is entirely on you. If you can't ask your mom to help you, then take the help that's available. Laurel wants to help, and Hudson has offered to let you use his parents' house. There's even a car for your use, and he'll cover whatever else you need."

"I don't want to depend on Hudson. I'd rather go to a rehab center."

"I've already accepted Hudson's offer." Susan placed his business card on the side table. "I'm spending the night with my folks, but I'll be here around noon to pick you up and take you to the service. I'll arrange for Laurel to get you back to Hudson's house, and you should accept her offer to come every day until you're well enough to drive. If you don't like these plans, you'll have to call Hudson and Laurel yourself." Susan moved to the door and stopped in her tracks, pressing her forehead against the wood. After a long silence, she turned back around and said, "I don't know what happened between you and my brother, but suffering in silence hasn't served you well so far. Please accept Hudson's help."

"You really want me to do that, even knowing that Hudson may have ruined Jeff's life?"

"Perhaps Hudson deserves some of that benefit of the doubt I just extended to you."

CHAPTER FIVE

The small funeral room reserved for Jeff's service was packed with gawkers and reporters. Hudson arrived a few minutes late, intending to be the last one in the room and the first one out. His jaw tensed when he saw Liv sitting in a wheelchair, a study in brittle dignity. Her left arm was still in a sling, and while her left leg was wrapped, the right was worse, braced to immobilize the knee. Her long, dark hair hung loosely, hiding her face until she turned his way. The telltale shades of bruising—blue/green and yellow—showed under her makeup on the left side. One stitched cut lay across the lean angle of her right jaw. Another sat above her right eyebrow. None of it obscured her beauty. She still took his breath away.

She remained poised through every speaker's measured remarks about Jeff's childhood and sports achievements, with a conspicuous silence on him as an adult. At the end, when the minster asked if anyone else would like to speak, Olivia raised her hand.

Several quiet moments passed after they brought the microphone to her. Then, drawing a breath, she said, "Jeff lived his life by William Arthur Ward's maxim, 'If you can believe it, you can achieve it.' So he lived as if he had already achieved the life he wanted—dreaming big, working hard, taking chances, paying his debts as he went, and sadly, dying too young. One hundred years ago, people would have applauded his spirit, and that is how those who loved him will remember him."

Hudson had never been more proud of her or more confused. By every measure that mattered, Jeff McAllister had been a lousy husband, but here Liv was defending him. Maybe she really did love him. Maybe their marriage was better than it appeared.

He left the room by the back door, but Susan zoned in on his retreat, broke ranks with the family, and caught up with him. She looked like a wooden soldier with her arms by her sides and her jaw as stiff as her resolve. Hudson reached out his hand to her.

"My parents are falling apart. I told Olivia I need to spend every minute I can with them. I sent you an email with the name and number of a friend of Olivia's named Laurel. She's willing to help out for a while, and frankly, Olivia has no other options. I've arranged for Laurel to bring Olivia to your house after the funeral luncheon, and then Olivia or you will have to figure it out from there. I'm sorry." Susan turned and walked away.

Flummoxed, Hudson pulled up the email and called Laurel's number on the drive home to hire her to be Olivia's caretaker for the next few weeks. As he ended that call, the phone beeped with a message from Alejandra, alerting Hudson that several gossip rags had picked up on Hudson's connection to the Jeff and Olivia McAllister story and had called for comment. He swore under his breath. The greatest miscalculation of his life and the resulting fallout were now matters of public discussion.

He focused on more urgent matters and hurried home to make things comfortable for Olivia, assuming she would agree to recuperate at the beach house. He was making closet space for her as a car pulled into the driveway. Nervous as a rabbit in a rifle sight, he went out to meet the women.

Laurel was standing by the open, rear car door that led to Olivia. After offering her a brief welcome, Hudson's gaze locked with Liv's dark brown eyes. The pain and fear he saw there made his heart lurch, and then a tear streaked down her cheek. She seemed as fragile as crystal. He longed to pull her into his arms and promise her that everything would be all right, but the fear of hurting her and the sting of her rebuke left him tentative and wary as he carefully lifted her into the wheelchair. Once Olivia was safely inside the house, Hudson turned things over to Laurel. "Settle her inside. I'll bring the bags, and then I should probably go."

PLEASE PUSH ME INTO A BEDROOM," Olivia whispered urgently as panic rose in her. Laurel obliged, pushing her down the hall and into the first room she came to. "I just need a moment."

"Would you like me to leave?"

A meager nod served as Olivia's response. "But please don't tell him I'm crying."

Laurel patted her shoulder, and then backed through the door, closing it.

Olivia surveyed the familiar room through tearful eyes. "The sunshine room," as Mrs. Bauer referred to it, had been hers on the many weekends she spent with Hudson and his parents. She remembered being awakened by the sun spilling through the large windows and the gingham checked curtains, bathing the yellow and white space with light. She could almost hear Hudson's knock at the door, summoning her for a morning walk while his mother prepared omelets and fresh fruit. They would work the daily puzzle between bites or argue over the day's news. She could often hear him belaboring his position through the door as she dressed. The room that launched those beautiful days, her sanctuary from college stress, caused her pain this day, serving as a reminder of lost innocence and of how far she had strayed from who she once was and what she once wanted.

She wiped her tears and took a deep breath. Jeff was gone. At their best, they were colleagues and occasional lovers. At their worst, they were masters of isolation. But even so, his had been the face she woke up to every morning. For eight years, they had shared tight quarters, broken bread together, cheered their few successes, and shared their disappointments. The tears began anew as she faced the blank pages of her future. They could have been more to each other. Could have done so much more for each other.

She needed to sleep. She needed her pain meds.

After a few frustrating minutes maneuvering the chair around the furniture, she managed to open the door but was wedged at an angle and stuck. With painful effort, she craned her neck and found Hudson and Laurel sitting at the kitchen table, flipping pages in the blue folder that held her discharge instructions.

She studied the intense worry on Hudson's face, his forehead resting in one hand as the other leafed through the notes. His face was leaner now, covered in dark, manly stubble. A few lines creased the edges of those dark eyes that seemed too intense for the once peaceful collegiate.

She could see the young man she once knew in his upturned nose and in the way he sucked his cheeks in when he was deep in thought. His previous thin, youthful frame was muscled and moved with confidence now. They were the same height—five feet ten inches. Back in their college days, she enjoyed wearing heels and towering over him. He never minded nor did she. He was now the one towering over others in the corporate world. No longer equals, they were worlds apart, brought together only by pity. Or by guilt.

She tried again to dislodge the chair, but the ruckus caught Hudson's attention. He rose and took a few tentative steps in her direction.

"May I help you?" he asked.

His formal address was uttered with a softness that melted her pride. She nodded.

So much about him was different. So much was yet the same. He had never cared for pretense. Comfortable clothes, serviceable shoes, soap, water, a neat haircut. These were Hudson's fashion trademarks. His style had evolved.

Hudson leaned over her to maneuver the wheels. The cologne he wore surprised her. Never a fan of guy perfume, as he called it, he acquiesced during a pre-graduation shopping trip to the mall. Olivia made him stop at the men's fragrance counter so they could test a cologne she found in the fold of a magazine at a doctor's office—Acqua Di Gio. She raved about the scent, but Hudson "didn't think it was him." She knew now that he had been right. This clean and woodsy scent suited him, taking her back to hikes shared with Hudson along the coastal trails, campfires on the beach, and the mingled aroma of woodland air and the sea.

The muscles in his tanned forearms tensed and rippled as he gripped the wheels and forced them to turn. His hands surprised her. They were not the soft, manicured hands she would have expected from a business titan whose daily work involved lunch meetings and business negotiations. They were clean, but calloused, marred by recent scrapes and a few healed scars. Hudson was still a hands-on man.

Once the chair was free, Hudson rolled her down the hall. She caught her first glimpses of the welcoming touches he had added to the house to ease her move. Three vases of yellow tulips brightened the bathroom sink, the kitchen counter, and the living room coffee table. She didn't know how to thank the giver standing behind her, the very man named in her pending lawsuit.

"The flowers are beautiful," she said, with a practiced coolness.

He replied with a detachment that was equal to hers. "Your favorite, as I recall. One of the first flowers in the Maryland spring."

Yes. Another thing he had remembered. He parked her in the living area, and she scanned the cheerful space. "I've always loved this house. Why did your parents move out?"

"These old wooden houses require a ton of maintenance. I

own it now and manage the upkeep so they can just enjoy it when they're here, which hasn't been much since they've gone to Africa."

"Do you spend much time here?"

"Not as much as I should, but I'm glad you're going to be here for a while. You spent a lot of time here before. One by one, we've all abandoned the place. I think the house feels lonely now."

Hudson's voice carried a sad, melancholy tone. The same feeling burdened Olivia's heart. She wondered if being here was the cause—in this house with its memories.

"I placed your bags in the master and moved my parents' things into the guest room. I also emptied my closet in case we need the other room for Laurel or the night nurse once we hire one."

"I'm sorry to be a nuisance."

"My mother will probably thank you. Now my college 'junk,' as she refers to it, is neatly packed in labeled containers and stowed in the storage closet with my elementary school paintings and my junior high shop projects. Her dream has come true at last."

Laurel giggled from the sofa.

"And Liv, the fridge is stocked with what I remembered as your favorites—vanilla soy milk, tropical fruits, and bread with as many grains as I could find. It feels like a brick, so it should be pretty healthy."

Liv … She hadn't been called that in years. Jeff had picked up on Hudson's nickname for her and referred to her as Liv when they were single, but he began addressing her as Olivia on the day she became his wife. She asked herself whether the change was meant to usher in a future with Jeff or to slam the door on the bitter break from Hudson. Olivia still had painful questions for Hudson, but this return to the beach house was also unearthing happy memories. as well.

"I should be going. I'll arrange for a night nurse, but I'm just a call away if you need anything."

"Can you stay?" The words escaped her mouth without thought, apparently catching Hudson off guard. His head tipped sideways, and he looked askance at her.

"You're asking me to stay?"

She immediately wished she could withdraw the words. "I thought we could talk."

He drilled into her with a look that seemed intent on extracting further clarification. Neither of them spoke until Laurel broke the standoff.

"I'll go unpack Olivia's bags," she said, as she veered down the hall to the master suite.

"I can stay for a while if you'd like."

"Could we sit on the porch?" Olivia felt his hands twist on the chair's handholds.

"Of course," but his voice sounded anything but sure as he wheeled her onto the deck to view the churning sea.

She tipped her head back, enjoying the sun's warmth and drawing in a long breath of salty pine-tinged air. Her heart relaxed with each breeze that riffled her hair and the wild ferns in the brush along the edge of the lawn. She studied Hudson as he leaned into the rail and watched the revelers below.

"Thank you for all you've done for me. For the flowers, for the gifts, for this view." Olivia looked down at her battered hands. "I'm grateful to be here and out of the hospital."

The rigid set of Hudson's shoulders relaxed as he turned

her way. "You're welcome. I wish you weren't in this situation at all."

She fingered her wedding band. "We have a lot of old ground to cover."

"No need to dredge up the past today. All that matters is how you are right now."

The sting of tears began again. "They say I'll be as good as new in a few weeks."

"No." The wistful reply was long and drawn out. "You'll be a new you. Hopefully, a happy you again, but your life has changed." He moved to the covered Adirondack chair near her and sat. "I heard about the baby. I'm so very sorry, Liv."

The words were right, spoken with an ache similar to her own. Hudson was also in pain, but was it from empathy or guilt? She muttered a thank-you and segued to a new topic.

"Tell me about you. What does a day look like for a business mogul? I can't picture you glued to a desk."

"Neither could I. I leave the day-to-day operation to talented software developers, lawyers, and MBAs."

"So what are your days like? Don't tell me you've taken up golf or something."

Hudson leaned his head back and laughed. "No golf." He gave a final chuckle. "I travel, looking for new talent and ventures." Growing more animated, he adjusted his position and leaned closer. "I've been to some of the most unforgettable places you can imagine, Liv, and met the most inspiring people. There is a wonderful, complex world out there, and it still needs dreamers and optimists."

Dreamers and optimists. "Doers." That was the term she and Hudson coined in their freshman year to refer to themselves. They were going to be doers who would tackle the great problems of the world.

"I don't know if you still have an interest in humanitarian work, but there are opportunities for you—when you're ready, of course."

His eyes sparkled as he spoke. Hudson not only remembered their plans, but it sounded as if he had been following through on them. The realization brought a pang to her heart. And then she remembered Arena Corp and the way Hudson cast her and Jeff aside. She was not ready to nominate him for sainthood yet.

She nodded. "Since I've commandeered your home, where will you stay tonight?"

"I have hotel interests in the area. They'll find a room for me or a utility closet somewhere."

An image of Hudson in a broom closet came to her, and in an effort to suppress her laughter, Olivia ended up snorting, which caused them both to laugh out loud.

"It feels good, doesn't it?"

"To laugh?"

His index finger stabbed the air, a token from a shared memory, their first real taste of the human cost of war. They had received news of the death of a college friend whose National Guard unit was attacked in Fallujah. For days, they didn't know how to appropriately distance themselves from their grief until one night when they were watching a movie with a scene that made them laugh. As if on cue, they stopped and stared at each other, each fearing they had sinned by feeling happy again. Liv started to cry, saying, "We're already forgetting him." Hudson's reply had changed everything. "No. We're just poking a hole in the sadness."

Liv poked her own hole in the air.

"Jeff would want you to be happy again. Anyone who loves someone would wish that for them."

A hidden message seemed included in his comment, but she was too weary and pained to sort it out or argue. "I hope you and I can find our way back to being friends again."

"I'm still here, just like before."

Again, a thousand unpursued meanings floated on that simple sentence. They each seemed to move back into their respective corners as they stared out at the sea, watching the gulls dive and sky-dance. She shifted in the chair in response to the increasing pain in her leg.

A look of panic overtook Hudson as he glanced at his watch. "I'm an idiot. You're an hour late for your meds."

He leapt to his feet and rolled her inside to give her the appropriate pills, with Laurel reading from the sheets.

"We need a chart to track your meds schedule," he said, as he pulled out his laptop and started typing. "I've contacted an online agency to hire a night nurse."

Olivia could feel him detaching, preparing the terms for his withdrawal. As conflicted as she was about him and his role in Jeff's downward spiral, he was also familiar, and somehow she felt safe with him. Once he left, her entire world would be reduced to one person, Laurel, a woman with whom she had spent less than ten total hours.

"Mr. Bauer," chimed Laurel, "Ben has to work late, and I promised my mother we'd pick Joey up by six. I can get him and come back if you can cover things here for an hour."

Hudson's voice softened again. "No, just go. You've been great. I'll wait for the nurse. And Laurel? Just call me Hudson, okay?"

She smiled shyly and nodded. "I'll work on that." She gave an apologetic shrug. "Olivia, I'll be back first thing in the morning before the nurse leaves. See you then."

The bang of the door echoed in the silence that hung in the room.

Hudson pushed back from the table and moved to the open kitchen area. "You're probably thirsty … or hungry." He opened and closed cupboards and the fridge door as he rambled off suggestions. "What can I get you? You always liked salad. And I have sandwich fixings. Or soup? We've got several kinds here—" He stopped and shook his head. "My menu is about eight years too old. Why don't you tell me what you like now?"

The choices overwhelmed her. For so long, with their tight budget in mind, she shopped for what Jeff liked, adopting his preferences over hers. She didn't know what she preferred anymore, and that realization unnerved her. "I'm not hungry."

He closed the fridge door. "You're probably tired. Would you like to rest?"

She felt pushed. Another man was "managing her." "Thank you, but I don't need you to wait on me. What I would like is a way to repay you for your help. There must be something I can help with. I would like a chance to work."

His face twisted in absurdity as he studied her braces and wraps.

"If I'm well enough to sit at a table, I'm well enough to use a computer. I'm quite good at programming and design, if you recall."

She hoped he caught her reminder that she was the one who brought his vision to life years ago. To her amazement, Hudson turned the memory back on her.

"Oh, yes. I remember." His response came in a slow, dramatic cadence. His eyes focused on an undetermined spot in the air, as if his thoughts were entirely somewhere else. Moments passed, and then his gaze drifted to her face. "I remember everything."

He turned to the sink and filled a glass, draining it with pained slowness, as if his thirst was merely a way to delay answering her request.

Calm had returned to his face by the time he turned back around. "All right. I'll bring a new phone and laptop for you tomorrow. If you're having a good day, we'll talk about work. I actually need to step outside and return some calls, so you're welcome to use my computer to contact people. Folks must be worried about you." He turned for the door then stopped. "You'll need passwords. The Wi-Fi password is my mom's name and my birthday—joan4386. My computer password should be familiar. It's KwanjaiThai4u. Use the numeral four and a small-case letter u." He exited and closed the door.

The password released a flood of memories that washed over Olivia. Food from the Kwanjai Thai restaurant fueled their brainstorming sessions while she and Hudson hammered out the details for the sports program. Whichever one of them picked up the food also delivered it, along with the "Kwanjai Thai for you" line spoken in a horrible Asian accent. The idea that he had hung on to that corny saying both touched and dismayed her.

Fatigue pounded her. Adding to her distress was something else Hudson had said. Folks must be worried about you … The error of that statement hollowed her. She and Jeff had mastered evasion to the point that she couldn't think of one person who would notice her silence for weeks. Her isolation was too much to face tonight. Gratefully, the doorbell rang; the night nurse Hudson hired had arrived.

Hudson strode in from the deck and let portly, middle-aged Nurse Maggie in. After exchanging pleasantries with her new patient, the conversation shifted right into business—charts and medical questions.

"I gave Liv her pain meds about an hour ago."

"Yes. I saw that in her chart."

"I can fill you in on her discharge instructions if you'd like."

"Is my patient impaired and unable to speak for herself?"

A flush of red rolled up from his neck to his cheeks. "N-n-no, ma'am. She's perfectly capable. I just thought—"

"Yes?"

"I suppose I'm leaving now." He nodded in Olivia's direction. "I'll be by sometime tomorrow. Rest well." And then he was gone.

WITH A QUICK GLANCE over his shoulder, Hudson realized he had been railroaded by a WWF-worthy opponent disguised as a nurse. He smiled and shook his head. Moments like these reminded him how unimportant he really was in the total scheme of things.

The humor was momentary, gone even before he reached his Range Rover. He sat on the leather seats and stared at the house, just now noticing how shallowly he had been breathing, as if holding his breath in Liv's presence had become his new normal.

First loves ... Everything the lyricists said about their

effect on a man was true. He felt like a wide-eyed dreamer in her presence. There were so many similarities to their college days. Once again she was alone, a stranger without a home. He wanted to shelter her, protect her. But that didn't appear to be what Liv wanted from him. She was an unknown now. Not just because she was widowed, hurt, and confused, but because of how she had left him in the first place and how she and Jeff had conducted their lives in the interim. Hudson wanted to believe that Jeff was the wizard behind the McAllister Marketing façade. He had a history of sabotage—bailing out on the first critical client presentation they had spent months setting up and then stealing the woman his supposed best friend Hudson had confessed to loving. But as unforgivable as Jeff was for his part, Liv had said yes to his instantaneous proposal, and she left without a word.

Maybe Hudson never really knew her at all …

He had built an impressive empire around helping people, but that required insulating himself from opportunists and frauds, almost never appearing socially and then, only in the company of his few trusted associates. He had met his share of false friends and conspiring women. He hated to admit that those experiences had left him mistrustful and solitary. Those unflattering characteristics could likely be about protecting the Bauer name, but they had also left him lonely and with a narrow circle of trust. And now there was Liv.

He reminded himself that he had come to her. She had not asked for him and in truth, made her dislike of him quite clear. So why was he hanging around?

An examination of the situation revealed that Hudson's pride was at the core. He would not be her crutch, but he needed to know a few things. Why had she set aside all they had been together, all he hoped to build with her, for a man who barely regarded her before asking for her hand? Had his judgment about Liv really been that flawed? That was the question that truly gnawed at him; a man who lived life more by his gut than by his balance sheet. And the bigger question pressing on him was, could he trust his instincts now?

CHAPTER SIX

Maggie, the night nurse, was efficient, professional, impersonal, and in charge. Olivia's meds were administered, her wounds checked, and she was readied for bed in half an hour. There would be no dawdling on Drill Sergeant Maggie's watch.

The morning also ran on an efficient schedule, with breakfast and morning meds at seven followed by bathing and dressing. With Nurse Maggie's encouragement and watchful eye, Olivia performed as many of the tasks as possible by herself.

As soon as the switchboards opened, schedules were set for physical and occupational therapy, but Olivia balked when Sarge tried to schedule recommended counseling.

The barrel-chested nurse softened for a moment. "You've lost a child and a husband, Mrs. McAllister. I know the pain of widowhood. I cannot imagine facing both. Please. Think about it."

47

A softball-sized lump formed in Olivia's throat at the mention of her losses. She knew she was compartmentalizing her grief, boxing it up to be faced another day after her body was healed. Perhaps that avoidance was why the idea of speaking to a counselor terrified her. She nodded her agreement to consider Nurse Maggie's request just to avoid the subject a while longer.

Instead, she chose to tackle what she could manage—work. After daring to check her personal email, which was devoid of anything personal, she opened the MMM email account and felt a sweep of pressure as unmet deadlines and printers' bills bombarded her.

She had designed this quarter's coupon, but Jeff handled the receipts, and he hadn't arranged for distribution before the accident. Their small business clients were depending on the revenue the ads would generate. The responsibility was now hers alone, and it was crushing.

Nurse Maggie rushed over and closed the laptop. "It's too soon for you to be working."

"I need to save my company."

"You need to rest that arm." She set a bowl of fruit before her. "Eat. Heal."

Laurel arrived and overheard the discussion. Her eyes widened as the night nurse reported on Olivia's condition and needs for the day.

Once the door shut, Laurel said, "Whoa ... she's intense."

"You have no idea." Olivia laughed and then sobered as she remembered Maggie's earlier counsel. "She pushes me. I think I need that."

"Then we'll follow her instructions. You look much better

today, by the way. Cute outfit too, but then again, you're gorgeous even when your face is purple and green."

"Yeah, right," said Olivia, as she twisted her long dark hair for comfort. She hadn't paid much attention to the navy-and-white striped tee and white knit slacks Maggie found in one of the bedroom drawers, but after examining them more closely, she recognized the quality of the fabric and noticed how they were designed to glide easily over her brace and bandages. She fingered the edge of the wide hem. "Hudson thought of everything."

"You must be very important to him," Laurel said quietly.

The comment rankled Olivia. "Hudson? Why do you say that?"

Laurel gave Olivia a sideways glance, noting her ingratitude.

"I mean …yes … it's incredibly generous of him to buy me clothes and let me live here."

"Well … yeah … especially considering that he personally packed and moved his own things into the utility room so you could have the master suite. But I was talking about how he stocked the house with your favorite foods and flowers. And you should have seen his worry when he read the notes about your injuries." Laurel flopped into a coral-colored overstuffed chair. "Ben forgets I have an egg allergy and nearly kills me with mayo every time he makes me a sandwich. He always apologizes and says he had other things on his mind, but I'm not sure that excuse is going to fly anymore. Consider what Hudson Bauer has on his mind, with his companies and charities and travels, but he still remembered all your favorites."

The breadth of his kindness suffocated Olivia. She had tried to compartmentalize each gift and service because the scope of his caring was more than she could bear. Yes, she needed some help, but the totality of his gifts was akin to placing a starving man before a gourmet meal. It was, in short, too much.

"I'd like to lie down for a while," she told Laurel, who rushed over to help. "And could you bring me that laptop also?"

Once she was set up in the bed with pillows propping her into a comfortable position, she went to work on MMM business. Within an hour her stress levels skyrocketed, and she closed her files, finding something on Hudson's desktop that intrigued her enough to compel her to snoop. The file name? Atmit Co-op. The link opened to a spreadsheet of universities and businesses partnering in the production and distribution of Atmit to refugee camps and villages across the globe. Links led to distribution schedules, reports of successes, and even a few letters from grateful tribal leaders.

She remembered a conversation the threesome had while sitting at a burger joint during their senior year. The topic was their Doer Campaign, but first, they had needed capital.

Everything hinged on getting a few Division One coaches to beta test their Arena Corp program so Hudson could accumulate data and she could tweak out the bugs before putting the software on the market. Jeff squawked when he heard they'd be giving their work away for months, perhaps years. It was then that Hudson expressed his definition of success.

He referenced an article about starving children in Ethiopia. Their bodies had degraded to the point that they could no longer digest most foods, but they could bear, and even thrive on a life-sustaining gruel called Atmit. The basic recipe was ancient—oat flour, powdered milk, sugar, salt—and with a supplement of vitamins and minerals, children near death could be revived and saved.

And the cost to feed a child for an entire month? Hudson had held up his double-stacked burger and shake. It was the cost of his meal. Six dollars. He said he would feel like a success if their program just made enough to save some children at six dollars a month.

Olivia felt like those children. Love starved, unable to receive more than the kindness equivalent of Atmit. But how could she tell Hudson that? Especially when she'd hired an attorney mere weeks ago to sue him for half of his company?

Her nausea returned.

Hudson had done it. He had followed through on his dream. He was a Doer. What had happened to her? She wondered if it was too late to find herself again.

THREE HOURS HAD PASSED when Olivia awoke. She texted Laurel, who came in moments, stretching and yawning, an embarrassed grin on her sun-kissed face.

"I feel a bit guilty about getting paid to nap on a porch overlooking the Pacific Ocean."

"Join the club."

Laurel readjusted the hair clips holding her brown curls away from her face. "We should do something nice for Hudson."

"What does one do to thank a billionaire?"

"I wonder how often he gets to eat a home-cooked meal. No man can resist good food with friends."

Memories of shared meals flashed across Olivia's mind.

"His favorite meal is barbecued ribs and corn on the cob. His mom had her own recipe for a sweet and spicy rub."

Laurel's eyes sparkled with excitement. "Ben is a grilling master. He'll be our cook."

"Do you think he'd help us?"

"Help prepare a thank-you dinner for the high school billionaire friend who's paying me enough money to make double payments on Ben's truck? Uh, yeah! He'll tell the tale for years."

Olivia laughed. She outright laughed, enjoying the stability of making a plan. Of having something to look forward to. Of having friends again. "We'll have to see how long Hudson will be in town."

Laurel nodded. "Okay."

The doorbell rang, and Laurel got up to answer it and Olivia followed in her wheelchair. "It's a delivery," she called back to Olivia. "A big box!"

The women watched the delivery man uncrate the item, revealing a strange-looking motorized wheelchair with wide rubber wheels.

"It's for the beach," said the delivery guy. He looked at Olivia in her current chair. "I assume it's for you."

"Wow," squealed Laurel. "Hudson thought of everything!"

After a brief demo, the man drove the unit to the back porch and parked it. Then he had Olivia sign the delivery slip before he stepped into his truck and drove away.

A sinking feeling hit Olivia. How could she accept another gift from the man she blamed for ruining her life? Could she sue Hudson and throw him a thank-you dinner? She rolled away from the table and over to the French doors that overlooked the sea.

Laurel stood and moved to stand beside her. "You look upset. What's going on?"

Olivia looked down at her hands. "You might not think much of me when I tell you."

Laurel sank into a coral-colored chair as Olivia wheeled around to face her.

"I've got a lawsuit pending against Hudson."

Laurel froze, seeming not to breathe or blink or move in any way. She whistled, long and low. "Does he know?"

Olivia's shook her head. "I just gave the lawyer the go-ahead a few days before the accident."

"May I ask why you are suing him?"

Olivia's eyes began to sting. "Jeff and I helped get Hudson's first company started, but Hudson cut us completely out the night we eloped. We were impetuous, and we probably would have ruined the chemistry of the team if he hadn't gone, but we deserved some compensation."

She wheeled away from Laurel and back to the French doors and the Pacific horizon. "Jeff and I tried to duplicate our previous success, but none of our efforts could recreate the magic we had when we were with Hudson. A few months ago, when I found out I was pregnant, I knew something had to change. I didn't want to drag my baby around the country, scraping a life together each month." She turned her head to Laurel. "I wanted what you have; I wanted a home. But Jeff said he didn't want children. He wasn't ready to take on a regular nine-to-five job and abandon his dream of landing a big deal. So I panicked. I searched the Internet and found an attorney who takes cases in return for a portion of the settle-ment. I asked him to petition Hudson for a percentage of his company's net worth."

"Wow." Laurel flopped against the chair back. "Did Jeff agree to that?"

Olivia shook her head again. "He didn't know anything about it until the day of the accident." She started to cry. "After leaving you guys and spending time with Joey, I was determined to convince Jeff to settle down and be a father."

Laurel handed Olivia a tissue, and she took a moment to pull herself together.

"He was furious about the baby. But when I told him it would be all right because I had filed a suit against Hudson, his entire face changed. He swerved the car to the shoulder and raved for about ten minutes. At one point, he twisted sideways and grabbed my shoulders. Something snapped inside him in that moment. He actually got tears in his eyes."

"I don't care about his feelings. Was he abusive to you?"

"Not physically. His weapon of choice was silence." She wiped her own eyes again and continued. "But this fight was different. Afterwards, he laid his head on the steering wheel and rolled it back and forth for a long time. I just sat there, worried he was having a nervous breakdown. Then he sat up, looked at me, and said, 'I can't do this anymore.'"

"This what?" Laurel asked as she leaned forward, closer to Olivia.

Olivia shrugged as new tears fell. "He just kept repeating that, and then he opened the car door and walked away."

"Onto the highway?"

Olivia nodded. "Across traffic. I think he was trying to get to the opposite lanes to hitchhike a ride away from me."

"And that's when—"

Olivia broke down again. "I caused this. I pushed him too far, and I've blamed everything on Hudson."

Laurel offered a half-smile. "I don't know anything about your past. It's just that … none of this sounds like Hudson. He doesn't seem very concerned about money, and betraying friends doesn't sound like something he would do either."

"No. No, it doesn't." Olivia's head fell into her hands.

"Call your attorney. See if you can put a hold on that suit."

"All my contact info and notes were on my old phone. I don't remember the name of the firm or the attorney's number."

"Oh, dear." Laurel went to the bedroom and retrieved the laptop for Olivia, who opened it and powered it up.

"I'll try searching the web for sleazy attorneys."

"It'll be like finding a needle in a haystack."

Olivia offered her a lopsided grin and nodded. "Then we'd better get started."

CHAPTER SEVEN

Forty-three text messages and countless emails were waiting for Hudson when he awoke in his hotel suite. He handled what he could from his phone, but he was both relieved and disheartened when the computer and phone he ordered for Olivia arrived by courier. She would now have the last things she needed. It was time for him to step back from her life and return to his.

He jumped in his SUV and headed for the beach house. It would be a quick visit, a chance to say goodbye before he returned to work. He knew he was fooling himself into thinking he could walk away easily and unaffected. But he had done what he could. The rest would be up to her. And the future? That would be up to her as well.

Laurel answered his knock and seemed startled by his arrival. "Oh! You're here!" She glanced back at Olivia, who Hudson could see was at the table, up to her eyebrows in a bowl of some concoction. Spread before her were spices and sugars. "We're, uh … just finishing up something before taking the beach chair for a test ride."

"Yes. Thank you so much for the chair, Hudson. It's … it's incredibly thoughtful," she rambled, as she blew an errant strand of hair from her eyes because her good arm and fingers were busily engaged in an attempt to hide the containers. When the hair refused to comply, her face scrunched, and she committed two reddened fingers to the task of taming it, all the while continuing the conversation. "We've been charging the battery for a few hours now." She placed a tea towel over the mess and wheeled herself away from the table and toward Hudson.

His knees felt like gelatin as he took in Olivia's present state—the fading blue-green bruises and two bandaged wounds on her face accented by a red spice mix splotch on her forehead that matched her reddened fingers. A mussed pony-tail framed her playful face, and his mother's now red-stained apron covered her like a shield. He felt his heart slam to a near stop as the moment transported him back eleven years. All that was missing were his parents and a stack of ribs on the counter.

His lips felt thick and sluggish as he tried to return her small talk. "You're very welcome." He glanced back at the table of ingredients. "Is that Mom's rib rub you're making?"

Olivia's shoulders slumped. She glanced at Laurel and said, "You've done so much for me, and by helping me, you've helped Laurel, so we wanted to make you a thank-you dinner. I remembered how much you loved ribs and where your mother kept her cookbook with the recipe for the rub." Her eyes grew wide, and she paled. "I hope you don't mind."

"No. Not at all."

"Can you stay for dinner tonight?" asked Laurel.

He remembered the evening flight he'd had Alejandra arrange. "Possibly." Did he want to get more invested here? A conspicuous silence set in before the gears of his mind began turning again. "I, uh, I brought a laptop for you." He carried it to the table and set it down beside his own. "Do you need to transfer any files before I take mine back?"

"No. Since I had reliable Internet access, I saved everything to the cloud this time, but thank you for letting me borrow it. Do you have a project for me? I'm ready to get to work."

His gaze moved to her restrained arm. "Are you really?"

"Yes, I am. Really."

"Okay. Then show me what you've got."

She straightened to her maximum height in the chair. "You're making me interview? You of all people know what I can do."

He sensed something more than pride in her response, so he dug in to see where the subject would lead. "You said you want to pay me back. Well, if you want to work for The Bauer Group, you need to interview."

Her head drew back. "I was volunteering to work on one of your humanitarian projects."

"Well, I'm offering you a job with a salary instead."

"You want me to work for you?" Her lips drew tight, and her eyes darkened. "So we've come full circle, right back where we began. Fine, then." She wheeled to the table Laurel had cleared and wiped down. Laurel handed her a clean rag to wipe her hands on; then Olivia turned on the new laptop. "Is the password the same as the one on yours?"

"Yes."

"Okay, I'm in. What task would you like me to perform?"

Hudson at least knew where her anger was aimed—at The Bauer Group. But why? He played on. "We're sponsoring some microbusinesses in Lebanon. How about framing a website for them?" He pulled a memory stick from his pocket and handed it to her. "Open the file titled 'Rashaya.' There are photos you can use. Dazzle me," he sniped back.

With her left arm in a sling, the work proved tedious, but she used a platform with pre-made backgrounds, and soon a tidy, functional site began to emerge. The resulting work disappointed Hudson, who knew that anyone could cut and paste images and links together to form a working web page. It took artistry to personalize a site, to evoke emotion in visitors so they became intimately invested. Liz had once possessed such skills.

Once her background was set, Olivia opened the photos of the refugees. Hudson watched her very visage fill with compassion as she studied each haunting image of survivors of the Syrian War. She chose several, placing them on the landing page, and soon the cold, functional electronic palette reflected the emotion Hudson saw etched on Liv's face.

Her work drew him closer until he was collaborating on the project. "We need investors and mentors," he muttered, thinking aloud to himself.

"So this is really a fundraising vehicle."

Her voice became as soft as velour, and Hudson knew the photos of ragged men, women, and children were responsible for the change. "Not exactly. Attracting mentors is more critical."

"Then we should use some of these other photos." She opened another screen and pointed to several images from the many pictured. "These characterize the people and their hand-icrafts."

"I agree," said Hudson, as he sat beside her, introducing her to the people in the images. "Their stories are all so compelling. You're bringing them to life, Liv."

He noticed the color warming Olivia's cheeks, and in an instant, he was eighteen again, working beside the awkward coed from his stat class. Her beauty and intelligence had not dimmed, but there was a new strength and grit to Liv now, and his proximity to her brought a return of the ache that sent him running first to Columbia University and then Mexico eight years ago, places that didn't remind him of, or smell like Liv. He dug his nails into his hand hard enough to cause pain, to break the spell and set his attention back on the screen.

An hour passed in a blink before Liv pushed back from the table to stretch her back. "It's coming along," she said, as if to distract attention from her physical discomfort. "If I can copy the files from that thumb drive, I'll have this ready for prime time in a few days."

Hudson didn't mention her obvious pain. "Go ahead. This is beautiful work, Liv. You haven't lost your touch. In fact, you've actually improved over the years."

She smiled up at him, then quickly pulled her eyes away, but not before Hudson caught the glistening there. Her desperation pained him. Her need for approbation. But what about her anger? He stood, needing to move away from her. "You're hired. I'll draft an offer and email it to you tomorrow."

She seemed startled. "Thank you."

"Great." He picked up his computer again and fumbled

with the power cord. "Then I think we're all set. You've got my contact info. I'll be in touch."

Laurel exited the kitchen space where she was puttering, and the two women exchanged worried glances. "Are you leaving?" she asked. "What about dinner?"

Hudson glanced at his watch, though time was not what was driving him to leave Liv's side. "I'm sorry. I really should make that evening flight."

"Then could you take Olivia for a ride in that beach chair before you go? She needs a practice run, and I need to get these ribs in the oven."

Hudson nodded, set his computer back down, and helped transfer Olivia from one chair to the other, reminding himself again and again that she was Jeff's widow. The woman who walked away from him. The loss that made living an agony.

He kept his distance as she fumbled with the controls, maneuvering the chair through the French doors and onto the porch. A winding trail led from the home's clifftop location to the beach below. Despite Hudson's vow to remain aloof, he set the controls to manual and walked backwards, guiding the drifting chair from the front while Olivia steered. With their faces inches apart, his resolve melted each time he looked up into her anxiety-ridden eyes.

At the bottom of the trail and slightly to the left sat the number one tourist attraction in the area—Haystack Rock—and its intertidal pools teeming with aquatic and bird life. The beach crowd was thin, leaving a few tidal pool enthusiasts seeking starfish, anemones, and other specimens.

The pair didn't speak as Olivia drove across the beach that spread before the monolithic sea stack. Hudson walked slightly behind her, suffering as they retraced the steps where memories were made, leaving wounds that remained as raw as when she'd left.

Olivia stopped when she came to a large outcropping of rock. "I love this place."

Hudson barely heard her above the sea sounds. Rather than reply, he stared at Haystack Rock, remaining silent.

"Do you remember senior year when the three of us came down here at midnight to collect specimens for your biology final? It was low tide, and we had the entire marine garden to ourselves."

Oh, yes. He remembered everything about that night in explicit, agonizing detail.

"Jeff said I could find lots of starfish in the caves, so I went because I wanted to surprise you, but the tide rolled in, and I became stranded. I was terrified."

Every muscle in Hudson's body tensed in latent anger. He shoved his hands into his pants pockets and steeled himself for the telling of the story.

"I tried wading back, but the current pushed me along like a cork. I thought for sure I was going to drown, especially when you ran back to your house. But you came back with a rope, hollering for me to stay put while you tied a line between one of the rocks on the shore and one near the Haystack. Then you pulled your way to me and back. You saved my life."

He felt the agonizing turn of the knife she'd inserted in his heart eight years ago when she married Jeff. Did she know what her words were doing to him? Against his better judgment, he fired one cruel shot her way. "And remind me where Jeff was during that rescue effort?"

"He was … he was here … on the shore somewhere."

"I believe he was laughing at us, as I recall."

Olivia grew thoughtful. "Why are you saying that? I was trying to recall a good memory between us. Why bring Jeff into it?"

"Why'd you bring this whole topic up at all? To preserve a memory? Then let's keep it accurate. For the record, you ran off a few days later and married the guy who let you down."

He could almost hear her heart shatter. Olivia recoiled and fired back in a cold tone. "I think we were all pretty good at letting one another down, don't you?"

He jerked back at the accusation in her voice, burning his eyes into hers until she shrank under his stare like wax in a flame. "How did I let you down?"

She took a deep breath. "I know we hurt you and ruined the team. I'm sorry. However naïve it sounds, it never occurred to me that you would leave." Several seconds passed before she turned to face him. "It just happened. I know it doesn't make any sense, but it's the truth. I knew how Jeff treated me up to then, just tolerating me. But on the night he told me he loved me; it was different." Her voice grew soft and oddly sad. "No one had ever kissed me or told me they loved me before. I got caught up in the magic of being wanted."

No one had ever told me they loved me before... The tender resonance of her voice read like a lie detector, confirming her words like the fatal testimony in a trial. *No one ... kissed me ... told me ...* Remorse slammed him for fearing Liv's attraction to Jeff but never having the courage to confront her about it. He had been a logical, tireless planner who misread the immediacy of her needs. Swallowing past a lump of choking regret, he shook his head and blew out a rush of air to silence his self-recriminations. "When was this magical, transformative evening?"

"Please don't mock me." Her head dipped, along with Hudson's self-regard. "It was June eighteenth. Jeff called me to come to the apartment to change the dates on all the presentation slides to the twenty-third, because the NCAA pushed the meeting date back."

The holes in the puzzle of lies began filling in for Hudson. "Did Jeff explain why I wasn't at this last-minute work session?"

"You were gone a lot at the end, Hudson. It didn't seem strange that you weren't there."

His jaw tightened. There was his other mistake. "So Jeff told you the meeting had been pushed back, and you and he were alone in the apartment, and he just asked you to marry him?"

She blushed and squirmed in her chair. "It wasn't quite like that. We took a break from work, and he took my hand and led me into the living room, telling me how important I had become to the company and to him. Then he left for a minute and came back carrying a big vase of yellow tulips. I just froze. He turned on the stereo, and 'Realize' by Colbie Caillat started playing. I remember getting goose bumps, because I had just mentioned the week before that it was my favorite song, and he scoffed at me, but there he was, playing it and asking me to dance." She rubbed at the goose bumps prickling her arms.

Chills hit Hudson also, but for different reasons. Icy chills that turned him cold inside.

"He was wearing Acqua Di Gio cologne. Remember how I tried to get you to buy some at that department store before graduation? He must have heard me talk about it. We were dancing but barely moving. He smelled so great, and he kept reciting the lyrics 'we could be perfect for each other' over and over in my ears. The next thing I knew, we were kissing. I had never been kissed before. Ever. Let alone by someone like Jeff …"

Hudson didn't hear another word after the phrase *someone like Jeff*, which replayed against images of deceit. He picked the conversation back up when he heard the word "friend." "What did you say?"

"I nearly died inside when we came back and you were gone." Her lips were trembling, and she pressed them together to still them. "You were my best friend."

Acid roiled in Hudson's stomach. "I'm sorry," he said, knowing he didn't sound sorry at all. "Remind me once again how I let you down?"

"We hurt you. We ruined our threesome. I get it. But you destroyed us. We helped you build that start-up company. We invested sleepless nights, missed classes, and we cheered each success right along with you, but you cut us out. You took everything and threw us to the curb!" As if to punctuate her final thought, she pounded her hand down on the armrest, evidently forgetting about her wounded shoulder. She winced and cried out, and Hudson took a step toward her, then retreated as she raised her hand, holding him back.

He looked at her, weighing every word, every vocal nuance. Did she actually believe this? He paced a few steps away and turned. His voice softened as he said, "I left an envelope. Did you read the note?"

She drew back defensively. "Jeff told me what you wrote."

"So you never read it. You trusted his word over every-thing you knew about me?"

"Yes, because I couldn't bear to read it."

Hudson's hands gnarled into fists. "We should go." He started walking up the trail.

"There's something else I need to tell you."

"Then I trust you can make your own way back to the house." He turned for the trail, walking on, listening to the weak rev of the beach chair's motor, hearing no crunch of the balloon-like tires over shells in the sand. And then the motor stalled. He knew the battery's weak charge was exhausted.

More than anything, he wanted to make a final, clean break, but he couldn't walk away, so he turned back around and found Liv frantically pushing buttons and wrenching the controls, all to no avail. Without a word, he moved the controls to manual and began pushing her up the steep trail. Soaked and sweaty by the time he reached the top, he pushed her into the house, transferred her back into her manual chair, grabbed his laptop, and stopped by the door, avoiding eye contact with Liv.

"Everything is in place, so you should be fine. I'll have an employment offer emailed to you tomorrow. Also, I've asked a friend of mine to stop by and check on you. Laurel, please let me know if you need anything." And then he was gone.

LAUREL WAS WASHING dishes when the pair stormed in. "What just happened?" she asked.

"I don't know. Did you see how cold he was when he first arrived? It got worse."

"What? Did you tell him about the lawsuit?"

"I didn't get a chance."

"You were gone for over an hour. What did you two talk about?"

Olivia shook her head in confusion. "I brought up an old memory from when we were friends, but he twisted it into an attack on Jeff."

Laurel pressed her fingers over her lips and remained silent.

Olivia blinked back tears. "I'm going to rehab as fast as I can and get my own place so I can get Hudson Bauer out of my life once and for all."

CHAPTER EIGHT

Hudson crushed the accelerator to the floor of his Range Rover, spinning out of the driveway in reverse and then forward onto the access road, drawing stares from the people he flew past. He longed for his old Jeep with the manual transmission, needing something more physical than the velvet ride of this automatic carriage.

A cyclist crossed his path a hundred yards ahead, and Hudson slammed his brakes early to avoid skidding into the rider, whose panicked expression startled Hudson back into control. The sting of shame bit his heart as he crawled the rest of the way through town, taking refuge as he stopped along a side street.

His head dropped against the steering wheel, then lifted as his fists hammered down in its place. He slumped against the seat and replayed the conversation on the beach.

He had blown it. Jeff stole Liv away, but her words also left Hudson charged and condemned. He had delayed too long in executing his perfect proposal, and foolishly, he had been absent too often after sharing his plans with Jeff.

The replay brought a new sting as Liv's condemnation returned.

We hurt you ... but you destroyed us. You took everything and threw us to the curb!

He pushed a button on the dash and initiated a call to Alejandra. Her familiar voice, with its Latin intonations, calmed him. And then he heard the worry in her voice.

"I'm so glad you called. I have been praying that phone would ring."

"I'm flying back tonight. Can it wait until morning?"

"No ... but I'll make it wait, and you'll owe me big time." He heard the increased Latin inflections that frustration introduced into Alejandra's voice.

"Thank you."

"Yes, yes. I make miracles happen. That's why you love me. So what do you need?"

"Everything on Arena Corp—the terms of sale and the companies we invested the profits in when we sold. Show me all disbursements related to that divestment."

"Arena? This is too strange to be a coincidence," she said warily.

"What? Talk to me."

"It's just that ... well ... someone else wants that information."

"Who?"

"I don't know, but they hired a sleazy ambulance chaser to get it. He's been hanging out at the food truck down the block, waving twenty-dollar bills around the interns' noses during lunch, asking them to dig up information on Arena."

Hudson felt the breath rush from his chest. "What kind of information?"

"Date of incorporation, date of sale, net worth at sale, reinvestment information. The very facts you're asking for."

"How soon can you get that to me?"

"Right now. I pulled all those files today."

"Are the investments purchased with Arena profits still going to the original owners of the company?"

"Yes. Nothing's changed. Quarterly transfers, like clockwork, into the same account."

"That we can't access?"

"Nope."

"There has to be a money trail."

"Maybe that's the trail the lawyer's sniffing. Speaking of the pin-striped pettifogger, what do you want me to do about him?"

"String him out, but give him what he wants. We don't have anything to hide."

"I don't like where this is headed."

"Implying what?"

"Stroll with me down Memory Lane, Hudson. The Arena Corp experience left you a wreck. All your business assets were in the Arena basket. The Bauer Group could barely pay the light bill when you hired me because you insisted that all the profits go to the McAllisters. When that Japanese software rendered Arena obsolete, I was almost happy to see you sell it for a dime on the dollar, because even if I had to sell empanadas on the corner to pay the rent, I was glad you were finally free of those McAllister leeches. But because you worried about Olivia, you turned around and signed the Arena profits, and some of your new assets, over to them as well."

"And the new investments paid off big, and we succeeded."

"But that scoundrel attorney isn't the only one digging up the past, is he?"

"I know what I'm doing."

"Do you? You love me because I'm the only friend you have who talks straight to you. Who benefits from digging up info on Arena Corp? Olivia. This McAllister woman is trouble, Hudson. It's too coincidental that this lawyer shows up at the same time she reappears."

"Or maybe she's a victim."

"Then tell her the whole truth and stop playing these games. Do you really want to face her in court? Because that's where this is heading."

"We don't know if she hired this attorney, but if she did and she stops the investigation on her own, she'll vindicate my faith in her character. And if she pursues it, I'll know I was wrong about her, and the whole truth will come out anyway."

"I don't like it."

"You'll like this even less. I hired her to work for us. I'll email the details to you. Make arrangements with HR to assign her to Ethan, and overnight an employment contract to her."

CHAPTER NINE

Hudson hadn't mentioned any salary figures, but when the employment contract arrived, the offer shocked Olivia. One hundred thousand dollars annually, with bonuses and full benefits effective immediately. She questioned whether she was hired on merit or if this was more of Hudson's charity.

As she read the terms of the contract, her opinion changed. This wasn't going to be any cushy forty-hours-a-week, work-from-the-sofa-in-your-pajamas job. The terms included international travel and stringent deadline clauses, which meant Olivia's hours would be crazy at times. She would handle it.

Excitement bubbled within her. This was a real job. A job that mattered and one she could do while she rehabbed. She didn't know what would happen when news of the lawsuit reached Hudson, but for now, she had the means to repay Hudson Bauer.

Her immediate supervisor was a man named Ethan Machowicz. She sent off a quick acceptance email and received a welcome email packet almost instantly that included a link to Bauer Group cloud storage files. Forms were signed and exchanged, HR was called, and within an hour, Olivia was gainfully and officially employed. Now it was time to get to work.

She opened the link and saw critiques of the website she had begun the day before. Ethan's feedback was positive and encouraging, and with a determination she hadn't felt in years, she pulled up the files from Hudson's thumb drive and dug in to make the requested changes and additions.

A file she hadn't noticed before caught her eye—My Girls. A battle ensued between her curiosity and her ethics. Curiosity won. The next click revealed seven folders and a video file. Six folders were labeled with the names of places mentioned in the website she was building, and included photos of Hudson with the woman and children from the thumb drive files. A folder labeled "Mother Thomasine" contained photos of Hudson hugging a thin older nun, of him laughing and singing with younger nuns dressed in white and blue habits, and in a school filled with African children. The man in those photos was the Hudson she remembered— joyful, hopeful, peaceful. She could barely tear her eyes from the screen. The video showed him in a circle of children, dancing and singing. None of this had anything to do with money. Something didn't add up, and she knew that the demon scapegoat she and Jeff reviled was of their own creation.

A shroud of guilt weighed her down, squeezing the breath from her. Laurel noticed.

"Are you in pain? Should I call the doctor?"

Olivia sniffed and blinked to clear her eyes. "No, no. I'm just stuffy."

"You have a doctor's appointment tomorrow for a recheck on your leg. And PT and OT begin in the afternoon."

"Sarge will have me up and ready at first light. After that, I'm yours to command."

Laurel laughed. "I wish Ben and Joey complied as easily as you."

The doorbell rang, and Laurel wiped her hands on a dish towel and hurried to open it. Olivia heard a female voice say, "Hello. I'm Dr. Sullivan. I'm here to see Liv McAllister. Hudson Bauer asked me to stop by."

Hudson Bauer asked me to stop by. The timing of yet another of Hudson's kindnesses was almost too painful for Olivia's repentant heart.

Laurel shot a glance back at Olivia, who answered, "I'm Olivia McAllister."

The iridescently red-haired, unnervingly toned woman squeezed past Laurel in a curve-hugging black pantsuit and red sling-back heels. She exuded confidence while sucking the last drops of it from Laurel and Olivia, both of whose shoulders grew rounder by the second.

"You can call me Pepper," replied the doctor, who snaked her way across the room, smiling at the Bauers' knickknacks and photos as if each were an old friend. Once she reached the sofa, she moved a white pillow aside and settled catlike into the cushion.

Olivia felt her hackles rise over the woman's intrusion into her … uh … Hudson's space. And what kind of professional has a name like Pepper?

"I'm sorry. Today is not a good day."

Dr. Pepper Sullivan remained glued to her spot as she fished her phone from her purse. "No problem. We'll just set up a meeting for next week."

Olivia rolled the wheelchair over to confront the woman. "Excuse me, but who are you exactly?"

Laying her phone in her lap, Pepper slid a stray hair away from her eye and grinned. "I am a licensed, Columbia University–trained psychologist, but more importantly, I'm Hudson's friend. My beach house is just a few miles from here. Hudson knows I'm there every weekend—Thursday afternoon until Monday morning. He told me about your accident and asked me to stop by to see if you'd like to talk."

The woman's overarching message—that she was very close to Hudson—outshone any offer of compassion. Olivia disliked the idea that Hudson had shared her private business with this woman, but she was even more surprised by how sharply Pepper's "friendship" with Hudson irritated her. Struggling to keep her voice even, she said, "I'll have to decline your offer, Pepper. You see, I don't plan to be here much longer, so my feelings and I won't be on your convenient drive home." Her voice broke at the end, and she turned away quickly.

Laurel strode to the door and opened it. "I think you ought to leave now."

Expectations of Pepper's exit and the door closing behind her went unrealized. Instead, silence passed, and then Olivia heard, "I am a very good therapist, Liv. Hear me out, and then you or I will know if this is going to work."

The previous icy tone in Pepper's voice warmed, but the

damage was already done. Olivia hunkered behind her emotional walls and pled, "Just go, please."

Pepper stepped closer to Olivia. "I owe you an apology. You figured out that I didn't come here to help you. I came to protect Hudson. I did a little research on you, your husband, and MMM. It wasn't flattering, so I wanted to meet you for myself."

Olivia spread her arms as wide as pain allowed. "Well, here I am, the guilty owner of a struggling business who was a wife in an imperfect marriage and almost a mother. I'm an absent daughter and a failed friend, but that is all I'm guilty of. Except to those who've believed the lies printed in the papers."

The color drained from Pepper's face and neck.

Olivia turned the tables on her. "And what are you to him?"

"I'm sorry? Him who? Hudson?"

Olivia faced Pepper without apology. "Yes, Hudson. I owe him a great debt, which is the reason I've accept his job offer. I intend to repay every cent. He's my employer. End of story. And I certainly don't intend to be investigated by someone he's dating."

Pepper's eyebrows arched as she stood. "We're not dating. I'm married." Her head bobbled, and then she corrected her statement. "Actually, I'm separated."

"But you love him, don't you?"

The woman's eyes widened and then narrowed. "You don't mince words, do you?"

"You're not required to answer. You're welcome to leave."

Pepper returned to her cool-as-a-cucumber persona. "My dating Hudson is not an option. Anyone who knows him also knows that married and separated are one and the same to him. Marriage is sacred. As you said, end of story. He's still a Boy Scout about things like that. About most things, actually. You, of all people, should know that."

Olivia found herself oddly comforted by the reply. Hudson was still a person of honorable character, and from what Pepper was implying, he evidently felt the same way about Olivia. That is, until he hears about the lawsuit. She groaned inwardly. "I'll take that as a yes."

Pepper pressed her bright red lips into a tight line. "Here's the long and short of it. Hudson sent me because he trusts me as a person and a doctor. We've laughed, cried, and consoled each other. In fact, we nearly died together once, but that's a tale for another day. So, are we good?"

"I don't know if I'll ever be able to trust you."

Worry creased Pepper's brow as she handed Olivia her card. "I'll never lie to you or run back to Hudson with anything we discuss. If you don't care to work with me, please promise to see someone else. I don't want you to crash and burn."

CHAPTER TEN

Four weeks passed quickly, filling nearly every minute with work or medical appointments or therapies of some kind. The heavy leg brace was exchanged for a lighter one, and the wheelchair was replaced with a walker and then a cane. Being mobile meant the night nurse was no longer needed, but it also meant that Laurel's daily company would soon end.

Olivia agreed to meet with Pepper. Their first session seemed benign enough, but Pepper raised questions that nagged at Olivia hours later, forcing her to examine long-denied feelings about her childhood and marriage. She finally peeled back the excuses and faced the truth about her one-day courtship and courthouse marriage. A one-two punch of fear and vulnerability set the stage. Jeff gave voice to her greatest fear—the possibility of Hudson moving on without her. Jeff offered her security, wrapped in smoldering looks and hungry kisses that overwhelmed her self-control. She saw herself slipping into her mother's emotion-driven pattern that first evening with Jeff. That realization sent her running back to her apartment, where she cried herself to sleep for being such a fool, but rejecting Jeff's advances only amplified his interest. He arrived the next day, teasing her with talk of long-simmered love. Her instincts again told her to run, but passion, and some other concern that now eluded her, over-ruled her hesitation when he dropped to his knee. An hour later, the couple was standing before a justice of the peace. And then everything changed.

Her face flushed with heat as she recalled how the bride and groom left the courthouse and headed to a sports bar where half the football team was waiting. How Jeff hung out with them instead of her. He was stone drunk and unsteady by the time they reached the downtown Seattle hotel where they spent their wedding night. There was fire and passion, and then the affection stopped. Aside from the peck she received at the end of their civil ceremony, she couldn't recall another instance where Jeff placed his lips on hers, and when she awoke the next morning in their disheveled marriage bed, Jeff's side was as cold as she felt inside.

She thought she had been used and abandoned until she heard the shower running. Nearly two hours passed before Jeff emerged red and weak, a haunted look on his face. His eyes were red as if he had been crying, but when she tried to comfort him, he turned away from her and asked, "How quickly can you pack?"

They arrived back at the apartment Jeff shared with Hudson, where her greatest fear was realized. Hudson was gone. The import of their decisions slammed the newlyweds.

An envelope addressed to Olivia contained Hudson's

parting words. Unable to bear reading it, Jeff did the honors. The words "I hope you're happy" had haunted her ever since.

Olivia shook her head and exhaled to banish the somber memories that crept upon her in the lonely hours after Laurel left each day.

Olivia was determined to earn her salary with her very best work. Ethan seemed delighted with everything she turned in and sent a constant stream of assignments her way —design requests, web pages, and logos for newly acquired or start-up Bauer Group companies. She wondered if Hudson ever saw her work and whether he felt his investment in her was justified. A month into her employment she had her answer when this email arrived in her inbox.

I received the first installment on your payback plan. There is really no need, but you may enjoy knowing that you are supporting an orphan school in Africa. Your work is incredible. I hope the rehab is going well. Don't rush to leave the house. H.

The note satisfied questions about her independence, her integrity, and her value as an employee. She wondered if the school was the one in the photos of Hudson and the nuns. She hoped to find out. Pleased, she turned in early, and while digging in the drawer for a nightgown, she came upon Jeff's wallet that Laurel had returned. Olivia had been unable or unwilling to look in it before, but she was now ready to explore the contents and face what pain they harrowed up.

She fingered the leather and drew in its scent. There was little sharing in their business/marriage, which created an unspoken agreement about privacy. They dressed in private and honored the sanctity of bathroom and shower times. Jeff never looked in her purse, and she never opened his wallet. Even now, she felt she was betraying some promise by peeking inside at the few small bills and cards. Her heart ached when she saw the handsome face and blue eyes peering from his license. Sad eyes. Women turned their heads to catch long glimpses as he passed. Such notice paid to him, and his quiet pleasure at receiving it, tore at her heart in the early days of their marriage. She had long since grown numb to such things.

The two debit cards—one to a joint personal account and another to their business account—accessed a sum total of barely more than a thousand dollars. She had since closed both and decided to shut down MMM.

There were no photos, no tender remembrances of shared times. Having removed all the contents, she still felt a lump. She noticed that the back liner of the bill area could be lifted, exposing a previously hidden compartment. Olivia peeled back the liner and found a small, well-worn blue envelope with faded lettering and depressions along the side. Inside was a key.

She had never seen the key before, but she was fairly certain it opened a safe deposit box. But to what bank in what city? They had traversed the entire country many times. And what could be in such a box, since they owned nothing of value?

Using the brighter kitchen light, she attempted to decipher the formal script on the envelope, but it was still impossible. She found a pencil and moved on to the embossed characters, rubbing the lead over the depressions until tiny letters appeared—BVB&T.

Nothing came up when she moved to her computer and

entered the letters in a search bar. Assuming the last few char-acters represented the words "Bank and Trust," she scanned a national list of banks that began with the letter B, with no results. The key was yet another mystery Jeff had left for her to puzzle over.

THE NEXT MONDAY, Laurel arrived in her signature perky way. "I took Joey to his kindergarten open house today. He is so excited about his fancy new backpack. Little things like that would have been impossible without this job."

Olivia smiled. "How much time do we still have? A week? Ten days?"

"Ten days, but I'll still visit, and you'll keep seeing Pepper every week, right?"

"Yes, but I want you to help me get independent. My phys-ical therapist said I need to walk longer distances before he'll clear me, so let's start hitting the beach."

"Good plan."

"And I can start driving soon."

"What about those flashbacks from the accident? Maybe you should tell Pepper."

She shivered at the mention of her recurring nightmare about Jeff's death. "I'm handling them."

"Olivia …"

"Okay, okay. I'll tell her, but I'm doing fine. Really. In fact, start coming later, like around ten, and leave earlier. I need to do more for myself."

"Are you sure? I'll email Hudson and give him my end

date. That means we've got ten days to get you completely independent."

"And to find a new place for me to live." She moved to her computer to search for apartments in the area. Instead, she found an email that made her shiver.

"Uh-oh. What's wrong?"

"I have an email from Larry Brewster ... that attorney I hired." She sucked in a breath. "Laurel, what if he contacted Hudson?"

"Just call him and see."

The phone rang five minutes later. Olivia paced with a slight limp as she listened to Larry Brewster's breathless update on the case.

"Some office interns are slowly giving us information, but they're reluctant, and that tells me we're on to something big, and big means we can expect a sizable settlement offer."

She felt she was about to be sick. "A lot has happened since I hired you. I don't want to pursue this anymore."

"Don't think about calling me off now. I've got hundreds of hours invested in this case."

"I'll pay for your time. Just send me a bill."

The tone of his voice instantly turned cold and calculating. "Then prepare to write me a check for a million dollars, 'cause our deal promised me a percentage of the settlement, which would've been substantial."

Olivia's legs began to buckle, and she slumped into a chair, bluffing back. "You've got no case if I withdraw my complaint. All you'll get is my fee for your time."

"Are you crazy? Do you know what you're throwing away? This Bauer guy is worth billions. You don't even need real dirt. He'll offer you plenty just to keep his name out of the papers. Don't grow a conscience now, lady. You wanted to nail this guy for ruining your life."

She could almost smell the lingering scent of stale smoke permeating his polyester suit. She pictured the chubby stub of a man mopping sweat from his brow as he counted his own potential fortune. They had only met once, but he was a person she would never forget.

"I was wrong. This case is over."

"Oh, the case might be over, but that just frees me to go solo. I know some tabloid editors who will pay big money for what you've already given me on the pious Hudson Bauer."

Olivia's hand moved atop her pounding heart. "Please don't do this."

"Hey, you're the one who started this. But thanks for the lead. I won't bother you further."

The man's voice echoed in Olivia's troubled mind long after the call ended. She turned to Laurel. "He's going to take the information to the tabloids." She could only see one option before her. She would have to speak to Hudson. "Where's Hudson's business card?"

Laurel found it behind a magnet on the fridge and handed it to Olivia, who called his private number. Instead of Hudson's voice, an elegant Latina woman answered the call. "You've reached the office of Hudson Bauer of The Bauer Group. How may I assist you?"

She opened by stuttering something completely unintelligible as she tried to organize her thoughts. "This is Olivia McAllister. I need to speak to Hudson, please."

A long pause preceded the woman's reply. "He's not available. How can I help you?"

The woman was a roadblock Olivia needed to barrel

through, but not today when she was still shaking from the previous call. "Please give him a message to call me. It's very important that I speak to him right away."

"I'll give him your message, Mrs. McAllister. May I say what this is about?"

Olivia noted that the woman used Mrs., as if she knew who Olivia was. "Please just tell him it's urgent."

She was still shaking when she hung up the phone. "I need to find a new place to live right away, Laurel, because you might not be the only one whose employment with Hudson Bauer is about to be terminated."

AFTER LAUREL LEFT, the quiet house only amplified Olivia's anxiety, so she kept her promise and phoned Pepper. She had to admit that she felt calmer afterwards. She was working on a project for Ethan when Hudson returned her call. The connection was poor, but even so, she could hear the worry in his voice.

"Are you all right?" he asked. "I was told it was urgent that I reach you."

She didn't know where or how to begin. "I'm all right, but I need to tell you something. It's very important." The background noise was so loud she could barely hear her own voice.

"I'm on a SAT phone on an airboat. We just pulled out from a village in the Philippines, and a storm is brewing. I can be stateside in two days. Can it wait until then?"

She didn't know how much time she had before Larry presented his smear campaign to the tabloids, but it was clear she couldn't have a conversation under the present circumstances.

"Yes," she shouted into the phone, "but please call me as soon as you can."

She thought she heard a confirmation on his end before the line went dead, but her anxiety ratcheted up as she imagined the conversation they would eventually have, especially if she didn't get a chance to talk to him before Larry initiated his blackmail plan.

And then the doorbell rang. She cracked the door open and saw Pepper standing there. The very sight of her momentarily lightened Olivia's mood. "You didn't say you were coming by."

"My new carpet came in early, so I decided to drive down, let the installers in, and finish our conversation."

Pepper's thoughtfulness touched Olivia. She finally noticed the neon-blue Spandex and running shoes the psychologist was wearing. "Don't tell me," she said when she opened the door. "The new plan to keep Portland weird is to dress up the medical community like glow sticks?"

Pepper strolled in and did a turn. "I do my best counseling while walking. A nice stroll along the beach helps us relieve tension and talk through our fears. After our phone conversation, I'd say we need a lo-o-ong brisk walk today."

Pepper's cut-to-the-chase style unnerved Olivia. "You make it sound like I'm an emergency case."

"You're more of a hider than a jumper."

Olivia was flustered as she left to change, and was still bothered when she returned, dressed for their walk. "You're bound by that physicians' code of confidentiality, right? You're not chitchatting with Hudson about anything we discuss?"

"Oohhh. Touchy. Of course not, but I do find it interesting that your first concern is Hudson, a man you can't stand."

"You're twisting my words."

"Am I? Have you decided that he's not responsible for ruining your life?"

"I jumped to conclusions."

"Glad to hear it, because he's the real deal, Liv. A good man. Someone who loves people, even when they don't deserve it."

Olivia paled. "I thought therapists were supposed to be caring and sympathetic."

"I'm not that kind of therapist."

"Clearly. Do your other clients respond well to this snarky nature?"

"Actually, they do." Pepper's characteristic sarcasm vanished. "Most of my clients are teens. I run an outdoor behavioral counseling program. We take troubled kids on high adventure outings and challenge them to work together and trust others, to push physical limits instead of chemical ones and see what they are really capable of."

A discomforting chill snaked up Olivia's back. "I don't need that. I just need to tackle my fear of driving so I can move on."

Pepper sat down beside her and took her hand. "We'll get to that, but I think you're afraid of a lot more than vehicles and traffic."

Olivia bit her trembling lip to still it. "Please don't dig up any more of my past. I've been doing really well lately. I just want to move forward."

"Liv, there is no true forward if you're always looking in the rearview mirror. You don't need to run from or forget the last eight years. Deal with whatever joy or pain they brought you once and for all. It's okay to be angry at Jeff or to dislike Hudson."

"It's not that simple."

"The very things you want to forget are the experiences that have brought you where you are, and in many ways, made you who you are—which from where I'm sitting is a very good person." Pepper's voice softened to almost a whisper. "Face your fear, Liv. You're brave enough to handle it and whatever else comes your way. You just need to believe that."

Olivia's gaze hit the floor.

"Let's stretch out those muscles before we begin, shall we?"

Pepper all but twisted herself into a pretzel while Olivia dared only lean against the wall to stretch out her calves. After a few moments, she broke the silence. "For the record, I don't hate Hudson."

"I know."

"Then why did you say that?"

"To provoke you. Confession is the first step to healing."

"I hate therapy."

"So did I."

Olivia's head shot around to face her. "You needed therapy?"

Pepper nodded. "I'm proof of what a few years of excavation can do for the soul."

Olivia rolled her eyes, and the pair headed out for the beach. Pepper pressed Olivia to talk about Jeff and their marriage, and then she raised the topic of Hudson and their relationship. Olivia talked and cried as they walked short distances up and down the beach to Haystack Rock and back.

When Olivia's legs grew weak, Pepper led them to a quiet spot on a downed tree to rest before returning to the house.

"Tell me what you're feeling right now."

Olivia knew that admission would be as painful as the conversation itself. She wrapped her arms around her midsection and bent forward.

"Being angry or sad or admitting that someone hurt you doesn't make you a bad person. You're allowed to make your own happiness a priority sometimes," Pepper urged.

Seconds ticked by as Olivia finger-combed her tangled hair, stalling. It availed her nothing. The redhead was a master at waiting.

"I'll tell you what. If you answer my question, I'll answer one of yours. Deal?"

Olivia nodded and blew out another rush of air. "Okay. Here goes. Jeff was always surrounded by beautiful women. I wish I knew why he chose me."

"You're also a beautiful woman, Liv."

She shook her head. "Not like them. I tried to mimic them." She chuckled sadly.

"To impress Jeff?"

Another sad laugh preceded a tearful confession. "I wasn't trying to compete for him. It was an experiment, a game I guess, to prove to myself that I wasn't an ugly duckling anymore."

"It worked. You caught his eye."

"That wasn't my intention. I think we each knew early on that the marriage was a big mistake." She raised her head and faced Pepper. "Why didn't he leave if he was so unhappy?"

Pepper placed her arm around Olivia and rubbed her back. "Why didn't you?"

"I don't know."

"Yes, you do."

Another groan of agony. "Guilt and pride, I guess. My mother married a man for security, not love. I didn't want to admit I had been equally shallow. Jeff and I were colleagues; he didn't love me like a man should love his wife. And I didn't love him." She fiddled with the handle of her cane. "And I'm angry at myself for staying in a marriage that made me feel like a disappointment. Someone else might have truly wanted me."

"There's plenty of time to make a new life."

Olivia blinked rapidly and took a long breath. "I've unfairly blamed Hudson. I had no right to be angry at him. We blind-sided him. We ruined things." The last admission drained her. She folded over her knees again and twisted her hair into a knot.

Pepper's voice lowered and slowed. "Are you truly being honest now? Because I think you were angry at Hudson. You just haven't been honest about the reason."

The comment sent a shockwave through Olivia's heart. It was true. She had been angry at Hudson, but not because he stole the company. It was for something too personal and buried too deep to excavate today. She rolled her lips inward and clamped down, ending the discussion.

Pepper's hand moved to Olivia's shoulder and gave it a gentle squeeze. "Don't feel guilty about wanting to be happy."

Olivia shrugged. "Your turn. You owe me one answer. Tell me about you and Hudson."

"I always pay my debts," began Pepper. "Hudson and I met at grad school in New York. I spent the summer before in rehab, but my parents thought a rigorous pre-med program would refocus my attention, and I was more than anxious to disprove their theory. Hudson had his own thing bogging him down when we met. We were two lost souls bemoaning life, who knew each other for about thirty minutes when we decided to throw in the towel, scrub school, and buy tickets for Mexico."

"Just like that?"

"Yep. Just like that."

"So what did you do?"

"We nearly killed ourselves."

Olivia gasped. "Suicide?"

"No. Stupidity. Equally dangerous."

Olivia straightened. "Wait. When was this?"

Pepper hesitated. "A long time ago."

"But what year?" pressed Olivia. "I was just trying to put this in context to when—"

"—when you and Jeff waylaid him?"

Olivia felt her face burn from a mixture of anger and embarrassment. "You know, you can be a real piece of work, Pepper."

"Just keeping it honest." She tilted her head to the side and offered a half-smile. "So, getting back to the story ... I slipped off on my own for an hour, found a dealer, and ended up wasted in some shack. Hudson scoured Puerto Vallarta for three days looking for me. He saved my life." She tipped her head back and stared at the sky. "He stayed holed up in a hotel with me during the terrible days I detoxed. He only left me to buy food and bottled water, but somewhere along the way he picked up bacteria and became severely dehydrated. He nearly died."

Pepper met Olivia's gaze. "It was so bad; he couldn't keep

anything in. His face was so hollowed, and his eyes were ringed with dark circles. I was terrified."

"So you took him to the hospital?"

She closed her eyes and shook her head. "I'm not proud of how I handled things. I was afraid they'd arrest me and toss me in a Mexican jail. Remember when I said he even cares about people he shouldn't? I was talking about me, Liv. Not you. I pooled all the cash we had left and hired a local nurse to take care of us. Her name was Alejandra."

Olivia recognized the name. "Hudson's personal assistant?"

"The same. She and her kids literally kept us alive. And she was tough. A day never passed that she didn't remind us of our foolishness and promise we would get well. When Hudson got his company going, he hired her. Next to his parents, Alejandra's the person Hudson trusts most."

"Followed by you."

"I'd like to think so."

Olivia regretted her absence from that list. "Where were his parents during all of this?"

"They flew down, tore into us for being so reckless, and brought us home."

"To school?"

"No. Back to Portland. Hudson's body healed, but the rest of him was a mess for quite a while." She looked up at Olivia. "We learned some precious lessons on that trip. I reapplied, got into med school, and switched my focus to psychology. Hudson launched The Bauer Group and hired Alejandra to help him choose good people he could trust to run each division." Pure love washed over Pepper's face. "Most amazing to me is that he forgave me."

Olivia's eyes teared as she watched Pepper's unabashed adoration. She knew every word was true. "You are in love with him, aren't you?"

The question didn't surprise Pepper. She tipped her chin up and raised her eyebrows. "Guilty as charged, but I figured out a long time ago that it was a fruitless position, so I did what you did. I married someone else, hoping they'd love me the way I wanted to be loved by Hudson."

The comparison caused Olivia to draw back, feeling as if her heart had been split open. "I never said—"

In true Pepper style, she switched from serious to playfully snarky. "Well, we've made good progress today, and the way ahead should be a bit clearer now."

Olivia knew that wasn't completely true. The day had only muddled her emotions even more. Trouble loomed for Hudson, and Olivia was the cause.

CHAPTER ELEVEN

L abor Day was lonely for Olivia, who watched throngs of happy families frolicking on the beach below the deck while she worked. She was grateful Ethan made her the lead on the Syrian Refugee Microbusiness Project. It kept her busy producing materials that supported the weavers, painters, potters, jewelry makers, and other refugee artisans. Helping these victims of war rebuild their lives was deeply satisfying work and one of Hudson's favorite investments. Working on it made her feel closer to him somehow and to the person she once was.

Ethan arranged for an October trip to Turkey, so Olivia and a photographer could travel to the camps to interview the new business owners. After rushing to get her first passport, a terrorist plot in early September forced the cancellation of the trip before the document ever arrived. For the first time, she considered the danger Hudson and his philanthropic team placed themselves in to serve the people and causes he loved. And she was now a part of that team and that threat.

Laurel's employment as Olivia's caretaker neared an end, and Olivia was about to be on her own. It was a daunting thought. Her mother had called the moves until the day Olivia boarded the plane for Seattle and college. The shy, nerdy coed connected with Hudson during the first week of school, and they became tied at the hip from that moment on … until she succumbed to Jeff's proposal and began a new dependency.

There were some exciting elements to being independence. She was employed and making good money, so previously unimagined possibilities were now available to her, but she was also the master of her future and solely responsible for it. It was terrifyingly intriguing. She needed Laurel to hold her hand through a few more firsts before launching into the world

Her back cried for a good stretch. Long, lean arms, tanned brown from all the beach walking she had been doing the last two weeks, reached high and wide as she yawned. A tender twinge here and there reminded her that she was weak and still recovering, but it felt good to be free of braces and wraps.

Two scars remained freshly pink on her forehead and cheek. Though healing nicely, they were daily, permanent reminders of the accident, making it hard to look in the mirror without thinking about the past and Jeff.

By the time her alarm rang, she was already up and dressed in exercise clothes—black yoga pants and a white T-shirt, with her straight, dark hair neatly corralled in a pony-tail. She counted it as a rather stellar accomplishment, since Laurel had rarely arrived to even find her awake. But this time, she was scrambling eggs in a bowl when the door opened.

"Well, look at you!"

"And I have a few ideas for today."

A broad smile stretched across Laurel's face. "I'm so proud of you." She pulled up a barstool and sat at the counter. "So … have you had any luck cracking the code on that bank deposit key?"

"No, and it haunts me. Whatever is in that box must be important if Jeff carried that key in his wallet."

"What if what you find there just causes you more pain?"

"Nothing can be worse than wondering for the rest of my life."

Laurel drew circles through a water droplet on the counter. "I suppose."

"What made you bring the key up?"

"Just curious. So, tell me about your plans. I thought we were going apartment hunting."

Olivia scrunched her nose and leaned against the counter. "Before I leave this house and killer view, I need to find a beautiful, peaceful replacement place I can go to when I need to have a good cry. Tell me about that place you and Ben hike into with Joey."

"Short Sands Beach at Oswald Park? Yeah, it's gorgeous there." Her hand stretched forward as if she were pointing to the places she was describing. "A white, sandy beach cove, forested cliffs, the tidal basin." She rested her elbows on the counter and leaned in. "There's this deep cave that sits near a waterfall that tumbles down into the tidal basin." A swoon broke as she closed her eyes. "I've had fantasies about going all Tarzan and Jane in that cave with Ben," she sighed, returning to reality, "but we generally go packing our five-year-old chaperone, so we search for starfish and anemones instead. No complaints. It's Joey's favorite place, too. Just off Highway 101."

"Let's go there today."

Laurel leaned back and eyed Olivia. "It's a half-mile hike along a mountain wall. I don't think you're ready for that."

"You take Joey there while wearing backpacks, so it can't be too dangerous."

"But Ben and I watch Joey every second, and his legs never tire. You've just been released from physical therapy. You might make it down to the beach okay, but it's all uphill on the return, and no cars can reach us if you wear out. It's hike-in-and-hike-out only."

"We've done two miles on the beach. Surely I can make a half-mile decline, and then I can rest. And on the way out, aren't there places to stop for a minute if I do get tired?"

"You stop and rest all the time on the beach. There are only a few spots on that mountain, Olivia. And only one pull-off to let people pass."

Olivia was already up and grabbing a backpack off a chair. "I found this pack in the garage. I packed two water bottles, grapes, and two sandwiches. Let's go."

"I ..."

She turned and shot Laurel a kilowatt smile. "Trust me. I can do this, Laurel. I feel great."

Olivia missed Laurel's anguished groan when she hurried out the door and into the driver's seat, waiting for her reluctant partner. Laurel rounded her shoulders in defeat, gawking at her through the passenger door.

"You're planning to drive? Down the highway? You've only

driven up and down the access road since the accident. Transition into these things, Olivia. I can come for a few hours next week, and we'll take things slow. Why be foolhardy?"

Olivia twisted the steering wheel in her sweaty hands. "I need to know that I can stand on my own two feet. I need to be able to get where I need to go, and that means I need to drive on the highway, not just merely downtown. I can't expect to be chauffeured around forever."

"This is a bad idea. I'll make a deal with you. Let me drive on the way to the trail, and you can drive back if you feel up to it. Deal?"

"All right, but I don't have a death wish. For the first time in a long time, I'm excited about life, but I want a full life. Not some anemic version of one."

"All in due time. Now switch seats with me."

The two headed for Highway 101. Olivia's breathing rate was still ramped up, and her heart pounded every time a truck sped by or a car passed. She hoped Laurel couldn't tell what was happening inside her in those instances when the image that flashed across the screen of her mind was the moment of impact between Jeff and the truck.

"The parking pull-off is just ahead," Laurel said with dread in her voice as she slowed and pulled in. A small sign confirmed their arrival at the trailhead to Short Sands Beach, but all she could see was a short stretch of dirt trail that disappeared into a thick curtain of foliage. She swallowed her apprehension and gathered her pack. With a bright smile of false confidence, she exited the car and waited at the trailhead for Laurel, who gave her a final, raised-eyebrow exit offer, which Olivia ignored as she moved into the woods.

A narrow trail, carved into the steep hillside, had been

denuded by years of foot traffic, but the slim path was the only claim man held in the forest. Thick roots pushed up from the path and jutted out from the hillside, making Olivia constantly veer over and around obstructions. After several awkward near trips and falls that brought her closer to the steep drop-off than she cared to be, she realized her ankles had weakened during her recovery and were unable to make the quick, nimble adjustments to stabilize her on rough terrain. To compensate, she tightened her other leg and calf muscles, adding to the fatigue already wearing them down. She found herself looking anxiously ahead for a break of blue through the trees or the sound of the sea above the hush of the forest. There was none.

The burn in her legs was joined by a jelly-like weakness that finally caused her to humble her pride and admit that she was in trouble. She leaned against the hillside to rest her legs. Before she said a word, Laurel was beside her, wide-eyed with worry as she assessed their position on the trail. "I'm sorry, Laurel. I should have listened to you."

"Never mind that now. We're more than halfway. You'll never make the uphill climb back to the car in your condition. There's a rest stop about twenty yards ahead. Let's get you there."

The words were comforting, but the fear trembling in Laurel's voice was not. Olivia nodded silently as Laurel took the backpack, placing it on her own back. She also moved to the front position, laying Olivia's hand on her shoulder. "Lean on me to steady yourself, okay?"

They set off again, with Olivia mirroring Laurel's steps over and around obstacles. After a few minutes, they reached a scenic overlook of the ocean where a bench was waiting.

Olivia bypassed the view, making a beeline for the seat, where she plopped down and bent over, breathing hard.

Her phone began to ring from inside the backpack, but she made no effort to retrieve it.

Laurel fished it out and looked at the screen before holding it out to Olivia. "It's Hudson."

Olivia shook off the information. "I don't want him to know—"

Laurel pressed the phone's button. "Hello, Mr.—I mean, Hudson. Really glad you called. We're in a bit of a—"

Olivia snatched the phone and sucked in a calming breath. She replied quickly with, "Hello, Hudson. What can I do for you?"

Silence preceded Hudson's confused response. "You called me the other day about something critical. I promised to call when I returned to the states. Remember?"

Olivia's brief recovery shifted into a new panic as she remembered the reason she contacted him—to confess the news about her pending lawsuit and to alert Hudson to Larry's smear campaign. When too many unanswered moments passed, Hudson began asking questions.

"What was Laurel saying before you took the phone? Are you okay? Where are you? I'm at the house and no one's here."

Cold sweat broke out over Olivia at the news. "H-How can you be here? You were in the Philippines yesterday. You said it would take two days."

"I hitched a ride on a cargo plane to California. It was easy from there."

Her shoulders slumped in guilt at her obvious ingratitude. Hudson must have altered his plans and rushed on, thinking she was having an emergency, and now, because of her impetuousness, she likely was. She kept making a mess of things, and the fallout somehow kept landing at Hudson's feet.

"Liv? Just tell me where you are and what's going on."

She choked back her rising emotions. "I'm fine, Hudson. Please don't worry about me. Just rest. We'll be home soon." Then she ended the call.

But Laurel took her own phone out and texted Hudson. After pocketing it, she shot an unapologetic look Olivia's way. "I'm sorry, but we're in trouble here. We need his help. He wants me to get you down to the beach. He's on his way."

Olivia did not argue.

The rest helped, but Laurel's steadying shoulder was required to help Olivia make it down the last hundred yards of steep decline. A picnic area greeted them at the base, and that was where Laurel deposited her.

"You're sopping wet and exhausted. Let's not add dehydration to the mix. Drink, drink, drink."

After Olivia complied, Laurel helped her hobble to the restroom provided by the Park Service, and then back to the picnic table. Exhausted in body and spirit, she lay down and drifted off to sleep.

CHAPTER TWELVE

When Olivia awoke, Laurel was gone and a scruffy, disheveled man was seated on the attached bench with his head resting on his arms, which were wrapped around a rolled blanket. Panic rose in her at the initial shock of the homeless-looking stranger, but she withheld her gasp once she realized that the stranger was, in fact, Hudson.

He was fast asleep, and it appeared that sleep was sorely needed. A thick reddish-brown stubble covered his face, and his dark hair was a tangled mop. Olivia wondered what he had been through to reach her and look as he did.

She reached out to gingerly finger a sweat-curled strand of his hair. Like a touchstone, the shared nearness shot a wave of memories through her. The result was a stark mix of joy and pain, happiness and sadness, want and anger. She withdrew her hand and sat up to end the thoughts. Her movement caused Hudson to awaken as well.

He seemed equally confused, clearing the sleep from his

voice and rubbing his fingers deeply into his eyes as recognition and welcoming filled them.

"You're awake."

"You too," Olivia replied with a dip of her head. "I'm sorry about … about all of this."

Hudson raked his fingers through his beard as he turned to survey the horizon. "A storm's brewing, and the rain will make the steep path slippery. That nap is the first real sleep I've had in thirty-six hours, so I don't think carrying you up the mountain on my shaky legs is a good plan."

"I could make it if I just had a little—"

Hudson cocked his head in incredulity, and she surrendered the notion.

"Help is coming. We just need to hunker on the beach until it arrives. There's a large cave down by the tidal pool and a fresh waterfall where we can refill your water bottle. It's the best option while we watch for our ride."

Olivia observed the steady stream of hikers and picnickers making their retreat up the trail from whence she and Laurel had come. "Where's Laurel? Did you send her home?"

Hudson nodded. "There was no reason to keep her from her family. Let's get you down to the beach."

He stood and tucked the blanket roll under one arm while extending the other to Olivia. She accepted his offer, fitting into his support as if it was meant for her all along. She leaned on Hudson more heavily the further they went until he was bearing the majority of her weight by the time they reached the ancient cave. Two surfers in wetsuits were exiting the cavern and gathering up their boards as Hudson and Olivia arrived. They, too, had their eyes on the darkening sky, but they shifted their attention to the couple and down to Olivia's legs.

"Sprain?" the taller of the two asked.

"More likely just muscle strain," replied Hudson when Olivia failed to reply.

"After we get our boards loaded, we can head back down and help carry her out."

Olivia stiffened at the thought of being hauled out by strangers like a sack of potatoes. Hudson made brief eye contact with her, evidently catching her mortification, and replied to their offer. "Thanks, but we've got it."

The shorter surfer glanced back at the dark cave and offered Hudson a knowing chuckle. "Gotcha."

In reply, Hudson shot him a look that ended his smirk, following up with a pseudo salute, effectually sending the dudes on their way.

Alone now on the beach, Hudson led Olivia to the cave, which bore the signs of frequent use. The sandy floor was clean and cleared of debris, except for the pile of rounded rocks in the rear, smoothed and carried in by the tides. Kindling and small branches were stacked near the cave's mouth, a few feet from where the remnants of someone's fire still sat in a charred circle.

Hudson untied the bedroll and several items fell onto the sand. Another good snap, and the blanket spread across the cave's entrance. Hudson lowered her gently to the soft fabric. Relief filled her, and she leaned back and nestled into the soft sand. Her sigh brought the hint of a smile to Hudson's beard-framed lips. It was short-lived. His face slackened as his dark, penetrating eyes fixed on her. His breathing seemed to stop, as did hers. Heat rose deep within her torso, spreading like fire through her face and neck from the intensity of his stare. A sheen of sweat broke out on her skin, and yet she shivered. She touched her face, expecting to feel the fire radiating there, but the motion seemed to break the moment. Without a word, Hudson took her empty water bottle and left, leaving her shaky and confused.

As he departed, she shifted to watch him pick his way through the primitive beauty of the area, around scrub brush, through the teeming tidal pools, to a glorious waterfall spilling from the rock wall.

Robinson Crusoe-esque with his rumpled clothes, his beard, and wild mop of tangled hair, Olivia was unable to tear her eyes from him. Gone was the shyness and gangly motions of his youth. The business titan who could buy or sell his own barrier reef or string of creature-filled islands now moved with confidence and care, as protective of a single mollusk or anemone as he had been as a beach-combing science student a decade ago. She wondered what made him that way. Clearly, the young man who had been everything to her back then was an even more splendid person now.

The all-too-frequent burn of tears hit her again. Pepper had been on the money. Olivia had loved Hudson in college. If only he had been the one to propose instead of... Guilt tore at her over the thought.

Hudson returned and knelt as he handed the water bottle to her, turning away to pore over the items that fell from the bedroll. They both seemed anxious to avoid meeting the other's eyes. With his back still to her, he spoke in a voice hoarse and low.

"I brought an analgesic cream to ... massage into your muscles. It should reduce the pain." He cleared his throat and added a thought in a stronger, more steadied voice. "Or you could do it."

Olivia's own tongue seemed thick as she replied, "I'd appreciate your help."

With his eyes planted anywhere but on her face, he sat, laying her calves across his bent leg. Gingerly, he slid one of her pant legs well above her knee and squeezed an inch of cream into his hand. In steady, even motions he methodically worked it into her muscles. The press and massage of his strong, warm hands along her knee and behind her thigh sent her heart pounding. Could Hudson feel her reaction? The concern caused her muscles to contract.

"Relax," he urged softly.

The firm, assured timbre of his voice caused the opposite reaction. Her muscles tensed in waves as images of the past crowded in on her. She set her gaze on the sea and tried to make light of the situation. "I caught the look those surfers gave us. It seems this place has a reputation, and they figured we were adding a new chapter."

A puff of breath escaped as Hudson chuckled softly in reply. "It's a family beach by day. But at night?" He shook his head. "I've heard some tales. That was never my style."

The melancholy in his voice caused Olivia to face him. "Did you ever find anyone special?"

Olivia felt the conspicuous halt of his hands. "Are you asking whether or not I've been in love?" His onyx eyes rose to meet hers and then held as he said, "Only once," in a pained whisper that brushed past Olivia's heart as if on torn butterfly wings.

Hers was not the only heart that had known the ache of rejection. "What happened?"

Having completed the massage of the one leg, he slowly pulled the yoga pants back over her knee and smoothed the creases from the fabric, making eye contact and again holding her gaze like a tractor beam. "Our timing was off."

The explanation gripped Olivia's heart until she couldn't feel the next beat or breath. She considered how many women he had met since her marriage. Beautiful women ... women like Pepper. The therapist said things hadn't worked out, but she had avoided sharing details about her relationship with Hudson. Had their timing been off?

Silence passed between them. Hudson dropped his gaze and returned to his work, raising the fabric of the other pant leg over her knee and working lotion into her sore muscles. Olivia could find no comfortable segue away from the moment. Gratefully, Hudson provided an unusual one.

"Did I ever tell you that my father's grandparents were Blackfoot Indians?"

She was mesmerized by yet another unknown aspect of this complex man. She shook her head.

"They moved to Alberta, so we didn't see them often, which suited me just fine when I was young, because they always seemed old and strange and poor. When I was fifteen, I discovered how wrong I'd been. My great-grandfather had passed, and Nuna was ninety-three and not well, so I was sent to spend the summer with her to help out. It changed my life."

Hudson elevated Olivia's leg and rubbed circles into a knot in her calf as he continued.

"She didn't have a lot in the material sense, and what she had frightened me at first. Her home was decorated with strings of beads, tanned pelts, and animal teeth, and she had the skull of an elk nailed to the wall across from her favorite chair."

"A skull?"

He nodded and smiled. "It scared me every time I entered the room, so I finally asked her about it. She said it was a love token, and that it reminded her of my great-grandfather."

He smiled as his gaze drifted over her shoulder to a spot on the horizon. Whatever he saw in his mind's eye caused his eyes to sparkle and glisten.

"According to Nuna, bull elk attract many cows, which they lead to good grass and to sweet water. The cows know their bull will protect them and their calves, even to his own death. These bulls became the symbol of a man's passion and love for his mate. Like the bull elk, a good man will provide for and protect his mate. He will build her a good tipi and introduce her to his family, where she and her future children will be welcomed and loved."

Prickles rose on Olivia's arms. Her eyes misted as Hudson listed every one of her dreams. "Your great-grandfather did those things for your great-grandmother?"

"Yes," he replied, drawing the word out like a pull of sweet taffy. "Nuna still felt his love every time she looked at the home he built her or rocked in the chair he made."

"That's a beautiful story, Hudson."

"It became very important to me. Perhaps because it reminds me what we can miss if we don't make the effort to understand."

Hudson's eyes held hers as if he were willing her to comprehend some cryptic message. After giving Olivia's leg a gentle, final squeeze, he drew the pant leg over her knee and set both of her legs back on the blanket. "Nuna told me I was like her husband, Black Moon. That when I found the right woman, she would see my love in the simple gifts I would bring her, and she would know my heart. I believed that. I may have counted on it too much."

Biting her lips to still them, Olivia coughed to stay the tremble at her throat. "Did you tell the woman that you loved her?"

His head shook in refute. "People throw the word love around so casually."

She considered her own desperate need for affirmation from Jeff. "It doesn't diminish the word's importance. Women need to hear it. We need those words."

Hudson's lips parted as if he were about to speak. Olivia tensed for his rebuttal, but he said nothing verbally. His shoulders drooped, his back rounded, and his neck retracted, bit by bit, until he was sitting back on his heels, thinking deeply, perhaps about what she had said. She felt her bravado weaken in the face of the compassion etched on his face.

"I'm sorry, Liv. You deserved better."

"So did you, Hudson." She sat up, rounding over her knees and wrapping her arms around her legs. Her chin moved back and forth across the fabric of her pants as she spoke. "I know we blindsided you. I'm sorry. School was ending. I didn't know where I belonged, and there Jeff was when I needed to feel loved." The memory and confession drained her.

She rested her chin on her knees and stared off at the far-reaching sand. "Every instinct told me he was playing me, but the need to be wanted won out. And then he showed up the next day, asking me to marry him. I was so confused. He said the way I kissed him back made him believe I felt the same way. It sounded as if I was the one who had used him. So I did what I thought was right: I accepted his proposal. And in an hour, the trajectory of my entire life changed."

She looked up, unable to read Hudson's expression, which seemed as veiled as the sun by clouds gathering off the coastline. The air suddenly changed as the wind kicked up and a low howl broke through the trees. Hudson jumped to his feet. Liv scanned the horizon to see if the gathering clouds had suddenly shifted into thunderheads, but the storm still seemed far off.

"What is it?"

"It's our ride. I need to signal to them."

The sound increased as he ran off to the center of the abandoned beach, but Olivia could not see a boat nearing the shore. The wind increased to a gale force, whipping the sand into a cloud around Hudson. She looked up and saw a helicopter arriving from around the cove.

As a basket descended from the chopper, Hudson ran back to her.

"I thought a boat was coming."

"This seemed the best option. Can you walk, or should I carry you?"

Her attempt to stand proved wobbly at best. "Can I lean on you?"

He spread his arm again, welcoming her in. Their eyes locked, and heat spread from her heart to her limbs. She forced her mind to put his kindness back into perspective. She needed help. Helping is what Hudson loved. She gathered more strength and independence as they made their way to the gurney-like basket.

Hudson helped her in and then signaled for the pilot to pull it up.

Panic set in when she began to rise. "You're coming too, aren't you?"

"I'll be right behind you."

Her hand gripped the edge of the basket, and Hudson's hand slipped over hers, causing the same firestorm to swell within her. He held on until he could no longer reach her.

"You'll be all right," he assured. "I'll see you at the top."

Fifteen minutes later, after a quick flight, they landed in a parking lot, where a limo waited to drive them home. Hudson limped more than walked by the time Olivia was settled in the house. She sat on the sofa and studied him. "You're exhausted. Go to bed. Use the sunshine room. You need to sleep."

He eyed her curiously, as if considering the offer. A moment later, he fell against a doorjamb and rubbed his eyes. "I can't. The driver is going to take me back to the pull-off at Short Sands to get my car. Stay here and rest. Promise?"

"I promise." The sight of him opening the door saddened her. "Will I see you tomorrow?"

He bit his lip as he thought. "Not tomorrow. Not for a few weeks, actually. I'm late for a technology summit in Tokyo, and then I'm off to Europe, but I'll be in touch to make sure you're keeping your word."

"Wait, wait!" she called out before the door closed behind him. "Are you saying you abandoned your schedule and flew halfway across the world to rescue me?"

He shrugged and shot her a lopsided smile.

The depth of his sacrifice began sinking in, and it overwhelmed her. "Your great-grandmother would be very proud of you. You are the man she said you'd be." Her eyes began to burn. "In case I haven't said it plainly enough, I'm sorry for all the trouble I've caused you. You weren't responsible for my regrets and unhappiness. My choices were. I hope you find your perfect match, that woman who understands your heart. She will be one very lucky woman."

Hudson stopped, his head tipping to the side as if considering her comment. He eyed her curiously from that spot as the storm returned to his eyes. Olivia caught herself leaning forward, willing him back in.

"What are your regrets, Liv?"

His voice was like suede, soft and masculine, inviting and warm. Losing Hudson was her greatest regret. She began there, unwinding that truth back to the reason she filed the lawsuit against him.

"I've told you about my childhood; how my mother attached herself to men she didn't love, all for security. She finally ended up marrying one my junior year. It was demoralizing. I always felt like a guest in that house, and I told myself I'd never be like her. That's why I wanted to get an education as far away from Diane as possible. But I ended up making the same spirit-crushing choices."

"You call your mother Diane?"

"We weren't like your family, Hudson, but I so wanted that dream. I attached myself to you, but I felt things changing between us near the end of our senior year, and there was Jeff." She looked away again. "In a knee-jerk reaction, after everything I'd done to be different from Diane, I ended up marrying a man I didn't love for security. But, here's the crazy part. I stayed with him to prove I wasn't like my man-hopping mother." She wiped at her eyes.

"I also regret drawing you deeper into my mess. I did something else that's going to complicate your life." She drew a deep breath and carried on. "Jeff made it clear early on that he didn't want children, but I was desperate to have something ... someone to love. There was such distance between us. I didn't take any precautions—"

"And then, that distance narrowed."

His crass assessment of her child's conception stung her deeply. "Please don't look at me that way. The baby was very wanted by me."

Hudson slowly crossed the room to her, his steps labored as if he were slogging through mud. He sat on the opposite end of the sofa, leaning forward, avoiding eye contact. With his forearms resting on his thighs, his hands dangled in the space between his knees. His entire body seemed wired. "I, of all people, would never judge someone else for wanting desperately to be loved, but—"

"You ...?" She scoffed. "Please. I've seen your photo on the cover of those gossip rags. What was the last headline? Weren't you named the man women most want to date? You're single by choice. You have no idea how lonely life can be."

His neck crooked at an angle as he shot her a quick, incredulous glance. "By choice? You think I had all the choices?" His voice was sharp and pained. He swore under his breath and stood, pacing to the door and back before turning toward her. "You can't absolve yourself of the damage you cause others by saying you just reacted."

Her head drew back. "What?"

"A guy who barely had a kind word to say to you in four years swept you off your feet in one night. That reaction was also a choice, Liv. A stupid one, but still a choice. And did you think to ask him if he wanted children? And when he refused to give you a family, did you leave? Staying was a choice. Did you wake up every day and choose to be miserable?"

"You don't know anything about my life."

"Only what you've told me, but I don't see where things have changed all that much."

"Wha—?" It was more a wounded groan than a word.

"When you found out you were pregnant, did you bother to see a doctor or did you just hope it would all work out?"

"How dare you!" She flew out of her seat and drew her hand back to slap Hudson, but he caught her wrist and held it firmly.

His eyes shone with pain. "What happened to you? What happened to us?"

"There never was an us. All I ever needed was a word from you, but you loved my work more than you loved me."

She spewed the words like acid, intending to inflict pain, and she knew she succeeded. He released her wrists and dropped his arms as he backed up a step.

"We were at least friends. I know about the lawsuit. Why? You said you blamed me. For what?"

Feeling as if she had gone nine rounds with a heavyweight, she dropped into a chair and curled over her folded arms, hiding her face. "I was desperate to give my child a better home than I had. A more stable life than the one Jeff and I were living. You wouldn't understand."

Leaning into the doorjamb, Hudson's voice cracked as he spoke. "You're the one who never understood. You said the woman I'd love would be lucky. That was supposed to be you."

She lifted her head enough to see him as a soft gasp escaped.

"I shared everything I treasured with you—my family, my home, my dreams, my heart. They were my expressions of love, but you threw them aside for a dance and a few well-chosen words." His voice broke with a sad laugh. "And the worst part is... they weren't even Jeff's."

A stabbing pain radiated through Olivia's heart. She pressed her palm against her chest to stave the ache as she processed Hudson's profession of love, mingled with his goodbye.

Hudson blinked as his head fell back against the wood. After a moment, he dug his fingers into his dark, knotted hair, grabbing handfuls. "I had hoped that someday ... maybe ... we could ... but ... I can't do this again."

She lifted her lead-like head at the spark of hope she thought he offered. "Are you saying you love me?"

"Do you really need to ask?"

She remembered the story about his great-grandfather's gifts of love, and how the right woman should recognize them. Olivia realized that by misreading Hudson's offerings, she had failed the test twice—then and now. Her bottom lip began to quiver. "Something changed during those last few weeks. The programming was complete, and you had customers lined up. Then you were gone so much and distracted when you were near. Jeff felt it too. We figured we had served our purposes and were about to be cast aside. Jeff offered me a safe place to land."

Hudson's hands covered his face and then dropped. "Of course he did. Because of me. I wasn't pulling back from you, I was winding up meetings and negotiations, building a future for us." He shook his head. "Maybe I seemed distracted ... by my fear. I was terrified, because everything I'd worked for meant nothing if I couldn't have it with you. I was gone that night because I drove here to pick up a b— ... something I made for you before I went to ..." He groaned loudly and kicked at the doorjamb, splintering the wood. "It doesn't matter where I was."

He leaned back against the jamb and slid to a crouch. "When I got back to the apartment, I found Jeff's note. I assumed you two were already off ... celebrating your marriage." The words came out like a curse. "One night, Liv. If you had only trusted in me for one more night."

All the air rushed from her lungs at the revelation. Neither of them spoke. Neither moved. Hurt hung in the room like bitter smoke.

He stood and kicked at the debris on the floor. "If you need the words, here they are. I loved you before I met you, from the moment you slipped through the library doors. You were so beautiful and frightened that first day. I watched you tug your hair as you scanned the room, looking for the computer stations, and then you flipped a strand over your shoulder and smiled. From that moment, I was a goner."

Melancholy filled his voice. "When Jeff got a scholarship to play at the University of Washington, he asked me to defer mine at MIT to help him make the transition. I consented, but I regretted that decision all summer until you walked in that fall. I arranged that study group and gave up MIT just to stay near you. And we were good together, or so I thought."

"We were," Olivia said softly.

"You believed in my dream and provided a sounding board for my ideas. That's all they would have been without you. But Jeff ..." Hudson gave one sad laugh and shook his head. "Jeff was only a mediocre college athlete, but he was one heck of a pitch man who could sell a line. I just never figured it would be to you. And you bought it on that night of all nights."

Olivia pressed her hands over her ears. "Stop. Please just stop, Hudson. It wasn't a one-night stand. You're picking my marriage apart."

The words stopped him cold. "I'm sorry." He took a step back into the doorway. "This thing between us … it's … powerful. It made me soar, but it also leveled me. No one else has that effect on me, but I can't afford to take that risk again. I need to go."

Olivia didn't understand what Hudson meant about a risk, but it didn't matter. Hudson did, and that was that. The finality of this goodbye was crushing. "I'll be out of the house tomorrow, and I'll turn in my notice to Ethan."

"Don't … please don't let this bleed any further. Move when you're well. And the job is yours. You've earned it and Ethan depends on you." He blew out a rush of air and shook his head. "Jeff was your husband, and you're loyal to his memory. I'm going to respect that. I won't bother you again."

Olivia rose and hobbled over to Hudson, but he shrank back when she reached for his arm. The pair were as tentative as shy teens with one another, standing apart, exploring every curve and feature on one another's face as if storing final images that would need to last forever. She moved to him, and he groaned a weak protest as she pressed her forehead to his. Tears fell as his arms slipped around her. She felt Hudson's frame shake against hers until she could neither swallow nor speak beyond the lump growing in her throat.

As bittersweet seconds ticked by, she took in his musky scent, cataloguing the feel of his stubble as it brushed against her cheek and the hardness of his chest as she pressed deeper into his warmth. Her hands slipped up, combing through his tangled mop of hair, clutching it in her fingers. Her head moved to his muscled shoulder, and his bent down, cradling her in the crook of his neck. They stood there, cramming a lifetime of squandered love into a few brief, haunted moments. His mouth brushed her cheek, sending shudders throughout her body; then, inch by inch, they found her parted lips. His hands framed her face, preventing her retreat, but she made no effort to withdraw, because this was the kiss she had dreamed of on lonely nights when Jeff—

Jeff—her body stiffened. The three short months since his death rewound in seconds, reminding her that she was a widow—and before that… a wife. A wife who loved another man! That was the source of her guilt. It was the truth that hobbled her. Jeff had not been the lone cause of their failed marriage. She had never stopped loving Hudson, and that guilt had cankered her heart, leaving her unable to love Jeff and unworthy to give herself to Hudson now.

Hudson pulled back, and she dropped her eyes to avoid him, but not in time ignore the depth of his pain. His hands slid down her arms and to his sides, leaving a chill over every inch of skin his touch abandoned. He stepped back, a fractured remnant of the man she knew.

Her voice was husky as she said, "I'm sorry. I just can't."

Shoulders rounded, his steps heavy, Hudson turned and walked out the door. Olivia watched numbly as his car drove away, knowing that this time he would not return.

CHAPTER THIRTEEN

He wanted to crush the accelerator to the floorboard and steer for the nearest tree. All logic and reason had fled, and for a few minutes, he didn't care about anything, least of all himself.

Like some heaven-sent beacon, Alejandra's distinctive ring sounded, but Hudson ignored it. Undeterred, she called back four times. He was ready to toss the phone out the car window when he saw her image come up on his screen. Her glasses were pulled down the nose of her elegant, portly face, and she eyed Hudson as if she were aware of his dark thoughts.

As hard as he tried to ignore the old memories, they returned—images of Alejandra's worried face hovering over him or sitting by his bedside with cold cloths and broth or of her delivering medicine and clean linen to him and Pepper while little ones clung to her hem. He took the call through the Bluetooth.

"Hudson—"

Her motherly "I-told-you-so" tone irritated him from the get-go, and he didn't make much of an effort to play nice in return. "How soon can a company jet land in Portland?"

"A company jet?"

He knew the extravagant request signaled trouble. "How soon, Alejandra?"

"I-I don't know," she stammered, her increased Spanish intonations signaling her worry. "You didn't order one, so other execs are using them to transport investors this week."

"Then lease one ASAP. I'm on my way to the Portland airport now. Just text me the name of the carrier and when."

Her voice softened with worry. "I take it things didn't go well."

"Do you want me to admit you were right about me and Liv?"

"I truly did want things to work out for you two, Hudson. If I didn't say it clearly, I'm sorry. All I've ever wanted is for you to be happy. You know that."

He did know that, and once again, Alejandra was reaping the bitter harvest of another rejection by Olivia. "I don't want to see or speak to or be recognized by anyone. Just get me a private jet and send me to Japan. I need to get back to work. I'm days late for that technology summit in Tokyo."

"Okay." Her worry seemed to intensify. "I'll be back in touch in a few. And Hudson, I'm sorry. I really am."

"Thanks," he muttered into the speaker. "And what were you calling about?"

"Nothing. It can wait."

"Don't coddle me. It'll be good to get my mind back on work."

"None of it's good news."

His jaw tightened and released. "Go ahead. What happened?"

"The rebels attacked the orphanage again."

The news of the attack on Mother Thomasine's orphanage in the Ivory Coast was like a splash of cold water. Hudson sat up and focused on the problem. "Was anyone hurt?"

"No, but they took everything."

"When?"

"Two days ago. Should I send more supplies?"

"Whatever Mother asks for and nothing more. We don't want to give the rebels a reason to return. What else?"

"The pump trial failed."

His shoulders rounded again. "How badly?"

"They collected a liter of clean water and then it died. You'll have a report in your inbox this evening."

He smacked the steering wheel and cheered. "A liter, Alejandra? That means the concept works. We just need to refine it!"

"Then God bless that liter of water if it can make you smile, my friend."

CHAPTER FOURTEEN

Olivia found her phone face down on the coffee table the next morning, next to the sofa where she had spent the night. On the screen was a long list of missed calls, all of them from Laurel. Olivia needed a moment to fully awaken, but reminders of the previous evening's pain returned. She wanted to shut the world out, but silence would send Laurel racing from Portland to Olivia's door to check on her, which would necessitate a rehashing of the very twenty-four hours she was trying to forget.

She sent a text.

Laurel, got your message. Thanks for calling. I'm home. Chat soon. O

"I'm here."

Still achy, she clomped to the door and opened it. The women headed to the sofa for a complete retelling of the ups and hades-level downs of the previous day. When the tale was told, Laurel moved beside Olivia on the sofa and patted her own shoulder. Olivia accepted the invitation, laying her head there.

"I'm so sorry. I knew Hudson loved you as soon as I saw the two of you in this house."

"It doesn't matter now. I don't deserve him. I blamed him, and then Jeff for my unhappiness, and I realized something ugly yesterday, Laurel. Jeff wasn't the only one who failed our marriage. I married Jeff, but I never stopped loving Hudson. What kind of person does that make me?"

Laurel reached a hand up to stroke Olivia's hair. "Don't you think Jeff knew how Hudson felt about you?"

"He must have. Hudson said Jeff betrayed him."

"And Jeff had to have known how you felt about Hudson."

"Hudson and I were together every possible minute, until the last few weeks of school." Olivia lifted her head to look at Laurel. "I think he was planning to propose to me the very night he found out Jeff and I had eloped. I ruined everything. I'm a train wreck."

"Or Jeff swooped in and pulled a fast one. Would you have accepted Jeff's proposal if Hudson hadn't been AWOL?"

"I can't pin this on Hudson. This was my choice. My mistake."

"But did Jeff feed your insecurities?"

"He first mentioned a change in Hudson about a week before the night he came on to me. I had noticed an increase in Hudson's absence, but I hadn't said anything until Jeff suggested that he was throwing us to the curb. We fed one another's insecurities, and we were both wrong."

"It all seems pretty calculated."

Olivia's shoulders dropped again. "Jeff may have been a lousy friend, but he wouldn't be the first guy to pull an end run against a rival. I'm the one who said yes, and now whatever chance Hudson and I may have had is lost. He can't keep getting bludgeoned by my problems."

"I still say those feelings are still there. When you're ready, you should contact him again."

They sat there, listening to the gulls' cries and the voices of vacationers below.

"I'm sorry for bulldozing you into the hike and the drive yesterday. Some friend, right?"

Laurel smiled and squeezed her hand. "When's the last time you had something to eat?"

"Hudson fixed me some soup last night."

Laurel lifted Olivia's head and stood, signaling the end of her friend's wallow. "Then you need to eat and take a shower."

Olivia waved her off. "Just go. I'm going back to bed."

"No, you're not. Shower and get dressed, because you're coming with me." When Olivia shot her a "no way" look, Laurel replied, "I didn't want to tell you this before, but I've got a lead on that safe deposit key of yours."

"You do?" Olivia straightened and scooted to the edge of the sofa.

"I was helping my parents sort through some old documents, and I saw their original mortgage. It was issued by Beaverton Valley Bank and Trust."

Olivia thought back to the letters on the deposit box key. "BVB&T!"

"Exactly! The mortgage changed hands several times, and the bank was sold at least once. It's now part of the big

Charter Bank Group, but originally, the bank was owned locally. And get this. Dad said there were a few branches back in the day, and one of them was in Hillsboro."

"Is that significant?"

"I think so. On the day of our picnic, Jeff said when he left us he was going to see his banker at the Charter Bank in Hillsboro. Plus, it's where we all grew up, so his parents might have banked there. It's a long shot, but I think we should try."

BOTH TELLERS at the small community bank were helping other clients. When a young teller with a name badge that read "Lynn" was free, she called Olivia and Laurel over to her window and asked, "Can I help you?"

Olivia removed the key from its old envelope and slid it across the counter. "Could you tell me if this is one of your safe deposit box keys?"

Lynn picked it up and examined it. "I think it is." Her gaze shifted to the envelope. "But our sleeves don't look like that."

Olivia's heart sank.

"But then, I've only been here a few months. I could ask the bank manager. She's been working at this branch for over twenty years."

"Thank you. That would be great."

Olivia and Laurel watched Lynn head to a glass door in the back of the bank, where she knocked and entered. After a few seconds, she returned. "Mrs. Bristol says it's ours, and that it must have been assigned way back before we merged with Charter."

Olivia beamed at Laurel, who gave a silent cheer. "Can we get into the box, please?"

A voice from behind them called out, "Just a minute, please."

Lynn rushed up to make introductions. "Mrs. Bristol, these are the ladies who own that key I showed you."

The fifty-ish woman eyed Olivia and Laurel. "May I ask who owns it?"

"I do," answered Olivia. "Rather, it was my husband's. He was killed in an accident a few months ago. His name was Jeff McAllister."

"May I see some ID, please?"

The lines along the woman's brow eased and then reappeared after seeing Olivia's license. "Mrs. McAllister, I'm very sorry for your loss, but I'm afraid I can't allow you to see the contents of that box. Your husband may have had a key to it, but he was not the owner, and I'm not at liberty to disclose who is. But, you are not the only person interested in those contents. A man named Larry Brewster was loitering in the parking lot the other day. He accosted Miss Cromwell here for information regarding your husband's accounts. I had to call the police."

The blood drained from Olivia's face at the mention of her despicable former attorney. "He accosted you?" she asked Lynn.

"He offered me five hundred dollars for information on all of Mr. McAllister's accounts. When I refused, he grabbed my arm, but I broke free and told Mrs. Bristol."

"I am so sorry."

"Do you know this man?" asked Mrs. Bristol.

Olivia hedged. "He was our attorney. I found him on the

Internet, but I fired him some time ago. Did you say that Jeff has open accounts here?"

"I'm sorry, I'm afraid I can't tell you anything more than that. You'll need to contact the owners of the deposit box."

Laurel looked crestfallen, but Olivia was not dismayed. She had a good idea who the owners had to be.

CHAPTER FIFTEEN

After saying goodbye to Laurel, Olivia placed a call to Susan. There was no answer, so she left a message, wondering if there would be a reply. Even if Susan knew about the deposit box, she had no loyalty to Olivia. No reason to answer her many questions.

The next two hours passed with Olivia curled in a ball on the sofa, rehearsing aloud her final conversations with Jeff and Hudson. Jeff was becoming an enigma to her as increasing mystery further clouded memories of their strained marriage. She tried to reclaim some thread of goodness from that relationship. One scene kept returning to her—the morning-after image of Jeff emerging from their bridal suite's bathroom red-eyed and bleary as if he'd been crying. His face was twisted in utter dismay. Was it because of guilt? Hudson's final conversation replayed.

I gave you what I treasured most—my family, my home, my

dreams, my heart—but you rejected them for a dance and a few well-chosen words … and … they weren't even Jeff's.

Jeff seemed to know my heart.

Of course he did. Because of me … I gave up MIT to make sure he graduated, and then my friend betrayed me.

Her emotions had been on overload. She processed a word here, a phrase there, doing exactly what Hudson had accused her of—reacting—and doing it badly. The conversation replayed in a loop, and now phrases stuck out. Something cryptic was hidden there.

I gave you my heart …

Jeff seemed to know my heart.

Of course he did. Because of me … empty words … they weren't even Jeff's … and then my friend betrayed me…

Did the words Jeff used to captivate Olivia come from Hudson? Her skin prickled as chills zipped up her spine. In her gut, she knew the answer. But how had it happened?

Another piece of conversation came to her from the day of the funeral, when she moved into the beach house.

And don't worry about my stuff … junk I should have thrown out after college.

She headed for the utility closet to look for clues. Seven boxes were neatly stacked. The top five boxes looked new, most likely the ones he recently packed, while the two on the bottom looked older, dustier, and more scuffed. These were labeled "2006."

Convinced she had nothing to lose, she moved the newer boxes and dug into the ones from 2006. The first box was filled with random things—photo albums, a photo frame, a scrapbook his mother kept of her only child's accomplishments, an academic letter sweater, and a few hats from their days at the University of Washington. She began searching through the scrapbooks and albums and was startled when she saw a photo of her and Hudson on the cover of a thin blue book that bore an elaborate graphic representation of its strange title, "The P³."

The image appeared to be a candid photo taken with a tele-photo lens. She knew Hudson's father had such a camera. The photo captured a moment that didn't immediately come to mind, catching them in the surf on Cannon Beach, their faces mere inches apart. Hudson's hand was near her face, brushing or wiping something from her cheek. Her eyes were closed, but it was the expressions on Hudson's face that captured her attention. Only a fool could have missed it—the captivating blush of first love.

Tightness returned to her chest as she sat on the floor and opened the blue cover to a five-page spread of photos of them together and titled "Beginnings."

The next two-page spread, titled "Discovering Your Heart," included photos of Olivia's favorite things: baggy sweaters, kiwi fruit, boat shoes, yellow tulips, a box of Andes Crème de Menthe, Acqua Di Gio cologne, Colbie Caillat's song "Realize." Prickles sprang along her arms and neck.

She opened the book to the next section. With tear-filled eyes, she studied the collage of photos he assembled to illus-trate their perfect date. The setting was classic Hudson—dinner on a blanket by the sea, surrounded by gulls, with a bouquet of yellow tulips, and Colbie Caillat playing in the background. Her eyes burned as she read the words printed along the bottom of the page— "Will You Marry Me?" Now she understood. The book actually was Hudson's perfectly planned proposal. "The P³." It was how he planned to ask her to marry him. She slammed the book shut. Except for the location, every element of Jeff's proposal came from Hudson's book. The morning's conversation returned.

Jeff seemed to know my heart.

Of course he did. Because of me ... and then my friend betrayed me.

She felt sick. Either Hudson had played Cyrano to Jeff's Christian, or Jeff stole Hudson's plan before Hudson had a chance. She knew the answer. She had been a silly, naïve fool.

With hands shaking, she reopened the cover and flipped to the final section, titled "Happily Ever After."

Page one was a copy of the letter finalizing the meeting to sign the contracts for Arena Corp. The date stung her heart. It was the date Jeff swept her off her feet and upset the balance in her world. The day before her wild elopement. What would have happened if the meeting hadn't been delayed?

The next two pages were a collage of photos Hudson had compiled—images of the beach house, three children and two dogs at play on the beach, and her favorite: his and hers computer stations set up on the porch overlooking the sea. Hudson's dream for them.

Tears dropped to the cover as she closed the book and reached for the photo. Hudson's beaming smile took her back to more innocent times when they were juggling schoolwork and the Arena project. She'd seen that radiant joy on his face once since then: in the images of him with the orphans and nuns.

She recognized the two older men in the image as Hudson's first Arena Corp clients—football coaches from major universities in two different conferences. Memorabilia on the walls indicated that this was taken in the office of Bellingham University's football coach. She knew that was the planned location of the scheduled contract meeting, and she assumed it was taken the night the contract was signed. But that was after her marriage, when Hudson was supposedly heartsick and suffering. So how could he be beaming?

And then a detail on the coach's whiteboard caught her attention. The date was written in the corner, and she felt ice run through her veins. June eighteenth! That date was the originally scheduled meeting date. On the night Jeff was supposed to be with Hudson, making the pitch, he had missed the meeting and lured her back to the apartment to work.

It was a lie. All of it was a lie. And she'd bought it.

Something else Hudson said returned to her. We both know he could sell a line. I just never figured it would be to you. And you bought it, on that night of all nights.

The depths of both Jeff's cunning and her weakness stole the very breath from Olivia. She sat on the floor with her back against the wall, unable to cry any more tears. Hudson had put all the pieces together, but she hadn't wanted to hear it.

What other secrets had Jeff hidden? She thought of the key, wondering where that would lead.

CHAPTER SIXTEEN

S he called Susan again, and this time, her former sister-in-law answered the phone. Susan's friendly tone stiffened once Olivia identified herself. They made it through all the stilted social pleasantries and questions of Olivia's health before the anticipated awkward pause set in, and then the conversation took an unexpected turn. Susan's voice softened measurably, and Olivia thought she even heard it catch as she began.

"I-I've wanted to call ... to apologize for the way I handled things. I was cold to you. Maybe I was still in shock. It's the only excuse I have. It's just that Jeff was my brother and my hero, and nothing about your marriage or Jeff's behavior made any sense to me or my parents. Anyway, I'm sorry for adding to your pain."

The revelations about Jeff's lies and his stolen proposal tainted Olivia's memories of Jeff, but Susan's memories were unblemished, reminding Olivia of the confident joker, the handsome swaggering jock that made coeds, including her, swoon. What had changed him so completely, so quickly? She hoped the answer was in the safe deposit box.

Susan's kindness stunned Olivia, who could barely find her voice to reply. "Thank you. It was a hard time for all of us."

"I've started to call you a dozen times, but I was too embarrassed, so I stopped. Could we visit sometime and talk?"

Olivia gushed, "I'd love that." Then a thought hit her. "But I don't know where I'm going to be living. I might move closer to Portland after all."

"So how are you and Hudson getting along?"

Olivia felt her heart clench. "He's been ... wonderful, but I need to make a new life and stand on my own two feet now. It's time, which brings me to why I called. I need a favor, Susan. Would you help me with something?"

"If I can. What is it?"

"I found a key to a safe deposit box in Jeff's wallet. Could it be your parents'?"

"I had completely forgotten about that. My parents arranged for that box years ago. They moved the summer before I started college, but they kept the safe deposit box and gave Jeff and me keys so we'd have access to the documents we'd need in an emergency—a copy of their will and our birth certificates."

"Do you know if Jeff ever accessed the box after that?"

"I have no idea."

"Jeff carried that key with him. There might be something personal in there. Something that could give us answers, but the bank won't let me open it, Susan. Would you open it for me?"

The silence that followed dashed all of Olivia's courage. She feared she had pushed too far when Susan broke back in.

"I'm checking my calendar. Work is killing me. It serves me right for being a know-it-all first-year teacher who complained too much. The benefactor of the school has named me the chair of The Pioneer School's advisory board. I have no life or free time."

"It sounds like they really trust you."

"That's great if I survive all this. So-o-o, I could come into Portland on the third Saturday in October. We could get into that box if we arrive at the bank early. Say, around ten?"

"Sounds perfect," said Olivia.

CHAPTER SEVENTEEN

The botched hike to Short Sands Beach set Olivia's recovery back and slowed her search for a new place to live. Once again, it was Laurel to the rescue. Now that Olivia was willing to relocate to Portland, Laurel felt comfortable offering the Ashburn's' finished basement to Olivia with a month-to-month lease. It would give Olivia time to sort out her life.

Pepper hadn't stopped by since their last chat, and Olivia's messages about her impending move went unanswered. There had also been no contact from Hudson, and Olivia's mind went to hurtful places, imagining Hudson finding solace elsewhere, like in Pepper's willing arms. She was stuck in an emotional crevice, anchored to a bitter past and unable to move forward. Her only peace came from remaining busy, so when she wasn't on the beach or spending time with Laurel's family, she was at her computer.

Work was increasingly more satisfying. Ethan had become

a true colleague who included her on video conference calls and sent her out to support clients in the U.S. He also began soliciting her input on projects to which she was not even assigned, and then she was summoned to The Bauer Group's New York headquarters for a meeting.

The excitement and expectation of possibly seeing Hudson flattened as her taxi crawled through the intimidating financial district. She looked down at her functional blue pantsuit and wished she had dared to wear something more sophisticated, at least high heels instead of sensible pumps. Her hand reached back and touched her long, loose hair. She pulled a clip from her purse and quickly fashioned her hair into a twist, but her confidence continued to lag.

She feared she was pretending to be more than she was. Less than a year ago, she was little more than a motel-room hacker, the Cinderella of programmers whose fairy godfather —Hudson—had placed in a dream job far outside her element and one for which she didn't feel qualified.

The taxi stopped outside a tower whose top five floors housed headquarters for The Bauer Group. Olivia took the elevator to the eighty-seventh floor and when the elevator doors opened, a man greeted her in a familiar, welcoming voice. Olivia recognized Ethan immediately from their teleconferences. "Security notified us you had arrived." Arms reached in her direction and grasped her shoulders as two air kisses graced her left and right cheeks.

"I feel as if we're already old friends," she laughed.

"You arrived just in time. Come with me."

Ethan guided her past the main reception area, down a hallway that ended in a blue marble wall where an eagle-eyed Latina woman sat at a desk. The impressiveness of the space, and the woman's instant dislike of her, assured Olivia that this was Hudson's office, and the woman was Alejandra.

Ethan ushered her to the left, into a glass-walled conference room where eleven people sat around a long mahogany table with their laptops open. "Everyone, this is Olivia. I know you're all familiar with her work."

Genuine welcome radiated from each face. Olivia nodded and smiled as everyone introduced themselves. Ethan opened the meeting with a brief synopsis of several upcoming assignments, which included another microbusiness project and a water project Hudson and The Bauer Group had been focused on for the past two years. In Ethan's words, "Sweet Water" had the potential to change the geopolitical future of parched areas of the world and, therefore, was a top priority for The Bauer Group, the WHO, and the majority of the UN General Assembly.

The name of the project struck Olivia immediately. "Sweet Water" came from Hudson's great-grandparents' legacy, the idea that a good man had a duty to provide this basic element of life for his family. Family. Olivia knew that was at the crux of the name. This wasn't a financial enterprise. This was personal.

After Ethan's intro, he turned to Olivia. "After reviewing the beautiful job you did with the Syrian refugees' microbusiness venture, we're all agreed that we'd like you to head up the new microbusiness project. We're calling it MBA—Micro-Business America." Olivia's heart sank. She so wanted to be on the Sweet Water project.

By day's end, three committee members were assigned to her team. After three brainstorming days, individual assignments would be made. Everyone would then go off to work independently, and Olivia would return to New York as needed.

When Ethan closed the meeting, he asked her to stay behind. Olivia used the opportunity to settle the question that nagged at her peace. "Tell me straight, Ethan. Did I earn this opportunity on my own merits, or on Hudson's recommendation?"

His brow furrowed. "The team reviewed your work and voted you in. Hudson didn't know I had chosen you for the committee until I told him. And for the record, no one else on the team knows you were Hudson's colleague at college."

"Colleague?" She forced a smile. "Is that how he described me?"

"And that you are a wizard of design. And he was right, but then again, the boss has always had a knack for hiring the best talent." He breathed on his fingernails and polished them against his shirt. "I wish you'd consider moving here. There is so much more I could involve you in if you were in-house."

The offer both intrigued and terrified her. "Maybe someday. I'd really like to work on the Sweet Water project."

"No, no. no. You can't do your best work on two projects. Especially while telecommuting. And the Sweet Water team may have to travel to Africa. No. I need you on MBA."

"Please, Ethan. I promise my work on MBA won't suffer. The idea behind Sweet Water is important to me. I don't need to play a large role. I'd just like to contribute."

He placed a finger on his lips and frowned. "Sweet Water is Hudson's pet project." Ethan smiled. "All right. I'll have the Sweet Water team assign you something small. Also, Hudson asked me to give this to you." He handed her an envelope bearing Hudson's HB insignia.

"What is this?"

"Rumor has it that it's a dinner invitation for two at five o'clock at the restaurant here in the tower. Now hurry!"

Olivia blushed red. "Thank you, Ethan. For everything."

A nervous excitement rolled over her as she gazed at Hudson's mysterious dinner invitation. She grieved again over her uninspired, sensible wardrobe, but she took a moment to brush her hair out and apply fresh lipstick before presenting her reservation to the maître d'. His eyes brightened at the mention of her name. He produced another envelope from a drawer at his station and handed it to her. It read:

Never worry that you are your mother. She possesses the same beautiful eyes, but you are not her. Enjoy your visit and see for yourself. H

Dinner with her mother? With her romantic expectations dashed, Olivia wanted to run straight back and tell Hudson off for meddling. Before she could make her exit, the maître d' led the way to an area by the fountain. Seated there, nervously toying with her compact, was Diane. Olivia wondered what her surname was now and what husband she was currently with. She studied her mother from the doorway, noting how timid and fretful she appeared. It had been almost ten years since they had last seen one another—Christmas of Olivia's junior year. Time was leaving its mark on Diane's beauty, but she was still what her last husband called her—a looker.

Diane pressed her hands over her mouth and gasped when she recognized Olivia. When she stood, she appeared small beside her stately daughter, requiring a stretch to reach her arms around Olivia's neck, and in return, Olivia bent to receive her mother's awkward hug. Diane's eyes glistened as she studied her, muttering, "you're so beautiful" and reaching for her hand over and over until Olivia begged her to stop and look at the menu.

The catch-up came quickly. Diane was still married to Peter Thibodeaux. The Louisiana plumbing contractor had opened her world, introducing her to NASCAR, Bluegrass music, and Cajun cuisine. She was even taking college classes.

Olivia redirected all questions about her past eight years, avoiding any discussion of Jeff. The last thing she wanted was to have her mother compare their choices and marriages.

"I can't stay long. I have a meeting back in the tower."

Diane's eyes sparkled with pride. "In this tower? Smart and beautiful. You're exactly as I imagined."

Olivia hung on the words. "You imagined me smart and beautiful?"

"Of course. You were destined to be beautiful, but I knew your smarts would be your ticket."

Tears burned Olivia's eyes. "I never felt pretty. I thought I was a disappointment to you."

Diane drew close and framed Olivia's face in her hands. "No, no, baby girl. I was the disappointment. I felt your disapproval, even when you were little. My momma valued beauty, and that's all I had. But I wanted something better for you, and look at what you've become: a successful businesswoman who can send her mother on a trip to New York City!"

Hudson had apparently arranged everything in Olivia's name, and she didn't correct the misunderstanding. Conversation came easier from that point on. When the pair parted, the hugs were genuine, and they made plans to meet again before leaving the city.

To her surprise, tears filled her eyes as she made her way to Hudson's office to thank him for making the arrangements.

Alejandra was still at her station, guarding the palace. She greeted Olivia with a smile carved into the concrete set of her face. "Hello, Mrs. McAllister."

Olivia froze and stepped back. "You know who I am?"

"I made your flight arrangements."

The explanation did not lessen the strange vibe the woman was giving Olivia. "I'd like to see Hudson, please."

There wasn't the slightest shift in the woman's expression, though Olivia didn't believe her when she said, "I'm very sorry. Hudson left for Bahrain this afternoon. Shall I give him a message when he calls in?"

Olivia knew Hudson's trusted assistant wasn't sorry in the slightest. "Please just tell him I said thank you." And without pressing further, Olivia turned and left.

CHAPTER EIGHTEEN

A gentle hand fell softly on Hudson's shoulder, momentarily drawing his attention from the street scene eighty-seven floors below.

"She just stopped by to say thank you. I told her what you said, that you were on your way to Bahrain. It's your fault I'll be going to confession this Sunday."

Hudson's pinched reflection looked back at him from the window. "How did she seem?"

"Happy. Content. You did a nice thing for her tonight."

He laid his hand over Alejandra's.

"You're a good guy, Hudson. Have I told you that lately?"

"Good enough to warrant some of your homemade empanadas?"

"Homemade empanadas? I'm a big executive now, with a very demanding boss. I don't have time to cook." She gave his shoulder a pat and walked a few steps away. "All joking aside,

I'm worried about you. You're here day and night. Barely sleeping or eating. You look like hell."

He turned to her and smiled. "Now you have another topic for confession."

"This woman isn't good for you. You can't afford to go back down that rabbit hole again. Too much depends on you right now."

He rubbed his fingers deep into his eyes.

"I see. You still love her, and you can't get those feelings to go away."

"I'm all right, Alejandra. Having her so close today was tough."

"As every day has been since she came back into your life. End this once and for all. Go to her and tell her you still love her. Get couples' therapy or call my priest to conduct an exorcism on you so you can be free."

He laughed. "I hadn't considered some of those options."

"I'm serious, Hudson."

"It's out of my hands," he answered brusquely, as he moved to his desk and slumped into his chair. "I'm sorry. I can't go to her anymore. Olivia has lived her entire life by other people's expectations. I'm not going to impose mine on her. She deserves the opportunity to become her own person. If that journey brings her back to me, I'll be the happiest man alive."

"And if it doesn't? Will you be able to survive that?"

CHAPTER NINETEEN

Two days after returning from New York, Olivia locked Hudson's beach house, severing this tie to Hudson and the past they shared. Closing her eyes, she retrieved a sweet moment, a final image to hold on to from those early days. Several bubbled into her memory and were quickly eclipsed by the memory of their final anguished goodbye and kiss.

Laurel, Ben, and Joey were the only bright spots in Olivia's personal life. Pepper sent Olivia a final text admitting that she had been wrong about her ability to be an objective counselor. She realized that her relationship with Hudson continued to get in the way. She sent several referrals, but Olivia never called any of them.

Rain and clouds cloaked her in a world as gray as her mood. Six weeks passed in a fog of work, broken only by time spent with Laurel and her family or at the gym Olivia joined. She missed the beach, but even without Hudson's house and his view of the sea, thoughts of him crept into unoccupied moments. Guilt always followed, creating a painful, unending cycle.

The day finally arrived for her visit with Susan and the long-awaited opening of the safe deposit box. Conversations over the month helped the women retain the progress they had made in their relationship. When Susan arrived, Olivia honestly saw her as a welcome friend.

Small talk on the way to the bank centered around three themes: Olivia's recovery, her new home, and Susan's work. The love Susan felt for her students was evident to Olivia, but when the conversation hit a noticeable lull, Susan asked, "Is Hudson still keeping in touch?"

The question seemed additionally awkward coming from Jeff's sister. Olivia stalled while she considered how to answer. "He was a wonderful support to me. He couldn't have been a better friend, but it was time for him to get back to his own life."

"Hudson is a good man. Did I tell you that I've always assumed that he's the benefactor who funded The Pioneer School?"

"How would he have even known you needed a new school?"

It didn't surprise her. Hudson's goodness caused another ache in Olivia's heart that hovered over the remainder of the ride to the bank.

Mr. Curtis, the bank manager, examined Susan's ID before leading her and Olivia to a private room. He left, and returned a few minutes later with a long metal box, which he set on a table. "I'll be outside the door if you need anything further."

Olivia felt chills snake up and down her spine as the door closed, and she handed Susan the key. For a moment, she questioned the plan, but before she could reconsider, Susan opened the box.

It was empty except for the items Susan expected—a copy of her parent's will and Jeff and Susan's birth certificates—and a plain manila envelope. Susan picked the envelope up, opened it, and removed the contents. A handwritten letter lay between a stapled document and a sheet of paper.

She looked at Olivia and down at her shaking hands. "It's for you."

Olivia recognized the handwriting immediately—Hudson's—though the penmanship was sloppier than normal. One glance at the first line, and she knew why.

I'll be gone before you two return.

Now Olivia's hands began to shake as she read the pleasure Jeff's friends—the wedding goers—took in delivering news of the nuptials to Hudson. And then she hit these lines:

When Jeff didn't show up for the meeting, I assumed he was sleeping off a party binge or with a member of his entourage. But you two? I never saw this coming. How long was I the stooge? I suppose it doesn't matter now. I can't see us working together going forward, so I'm giving you two Arena Corp as a wedding gift. I owe it to our investors to make sure it succeeds, but after a year, I'll bow out. My attorney will make transfer arrangements. I guess there's nothing left to say except, be happy, Liv. That's all I've ever wanted for you.

Hudson

The shaking moved into her legs. Olivia leaned into the table to steady herself while the information in the letter sank in. "Hudson gave us Arena Corp."

"What?" Susan picked up the stapled pages. "Yes, he did. Here are the documents." She scanned several pages. "They were signed by Jeff through a proxy in 2009, and the company was sold in 2011." Susan's head cocked to the side. "You didn't know this?"

"No. I didn't know a lot of things. How could Jeff have kept this from me?"

Susan sat heavily into a chair. "Where did the money go?"

"I have no idea. It didn't come to us." She remembered Hudson's allusion to Jeff's secrets. "Hudson knew. Why didn't he tell me?"

"Jeff was with you every day. How could he own a fortune and live like—" She caught the pain in Olivia's face over the reference to their lifestyle. "I'm sorry, Olivia. None of this makes any sense. There has to be an explanation. Maybe he wasn't husband of the year, but neither was he deceitful. I just can't wrap my mind around this."

Olivia reached over and picked up the last piece of paper. It was blank except for a series of letters and numbers written in Jeff's hand. "Another mystery. I can't take any more." Tears streaked down her face as she dropped her head into her hands. A sense of frailty overtook Olivia, as if her entire world was made of sand. Wringing her hands, she said, "I need to get out of here. I can't think about this right now."

The women closed the box and opened the door, finding the bank manager standing near.

"Is there anything else I can do for you ladies?"

"No, thank you," Olivia managed to say. "We appreciate your help." As she beelined for the exit, Susan turned back to the man.

"Could you take a look at something for us? Olivia, can I show him the numbers?"

Olivia handed Susan the sheet.

"Do these letters and numbers mean anything to you?"

asked Susan. "They belonged to a man named Jeff McAllister. He passed away several months ago. Does that name ring a bell?"

The banker studied the paper and bit the side of his cheek. "I believe this series follows Switzerland's IBAN, or International Bank Account Number format." He pointed to the string of characters. "The 'C' and 'H' here are the country code for Switzerland. The rest of these numbers are in the right order and of the correct length to identify a bank and an account, but you'd need someone to run it through an IBAN validation program to verify its authenticity."

"Could you?" Susan stopped herself and turned to Olivia. "I'm sorry. It's your call."

Olivia nodded. "Please. Would you do it? We'd both like to know."

He left for a few minutes and returned with an apologetic smile. "I thought I remembered the name Jeff McAllister, but I needed to be sure. Six or seven years ago, Mr. McAllister made an appointment with me, asking me to recommend a Swiss bank. I did my research and called him back, suggesting Zurich Cantonal, which another of our clients uses. That's all I know. Mr. McAllister contacted them and made all the financial arrangements himself."

"So he really did it," said Olivia flatly, as the chaos and betrayal rushed back in.

Susan's eyes welled up. "Mr. Curtis, can we access that account? We need answers."

"Did he have a will?"

The women looked at one another and shook their heads. "He died in an accident," said Olivia. "Wills just didn't seem important to a man of thirty."

Mr. Curtis's face softened with understanding. "I do understand. However, I'm afraid Mr. McAllister's passing, the international nature of this account, and the absence of a will complicates matters considerably. You need a good attorney to sort this out."

Olivia thanked the man, grabbed Susan's hand, and pulled her through the front door as her mind wrestled with an increasing list of questions. There was money she never knew about. Money from Arena Corp. Money they could have built a life with. Why had Jeff kept it secret?

"Do you have a good attorney?"

"That depends on your definition of good." Olivia did know an attorney, a sleazebag who knew how to bend the rules to get information, and Larry Brewster owed her.

CHAPTER TWENTY

Susan sat on the sofa, biting her fingernail as Olivia lowered herself into a chair and dialed Larry Brewster's number. She set the call on speaker.

"Larry Brewster here."

"Mr. Brewster, this is Olivia McAllister."

His groan echoed in her ear. "Geez, lady, you've got no beef with me. The way I figure it, you owe me."

"How do you figure that?"

"I gave up investigating your Mr. Bauer. He's so clean he probably squeaks when he walks. But you already knew that, so tell me why you led me on a wild goose chase with those claims that he stole that company out from under you? I saw those transfer-of-ownership papers. Your name and your husband's were all over that document."

"How could you possibly have seen those papers? I just found out about them."

"It's what I do. I slipped one of Hudson Bauer's employees a hundred spot, and she gave me a peek."

"But I never saw or signed any papers about Arena Corp."

"Did your husband ever ask you to sign a proxy doc? Seven or eight years ago?"

She thought back to a night near their anniversary when Jeff took her out to a restaurant. Before dessert, he slid papers and a pen her way for her to sign. Humiliation hit her like a spray of ice water over the memory. She had been such a weak, spineless fool, so grateful for his attention that she asked few questions. "Yes," she replied in defeat. "He said he was opening an account."

"That's an understatement. You never read the document?"

"No."

Susan stood up and walked to a window. Olivia's heart broke for her.

"I take it you never saw any revenue from the company either."

She grasped at a final straw. "Maybe there wasn't any. I heard the company failed."

"But it was worth over two million dollars when Bauer signed it over at the end of its first year. A Japanese program took over the market, so the management company sold the stock and invested it in other tech industries. Your husband had to have been making the final decisions. There's money. Somewhere."

Olivia's eyes began to sting.

"So you're telling me you have absolutely no knowledge of Arena Corp?"

"I might have something. Jeff opened a Swiss bank

account. It might be attached to the business, but my name isn't on it. Can you get access to that account?"

"It'll take some doing, but unless some other person or entity is attached to that account, the money should legally go to you. But once the case goes international, my price goes way up."

"I'm sure we can agree on something fair. You run a sleazy operation, Mr. Brewster. I didn't know that when I hired you. In truth, though, I was on your level at the time. I'm giving us both a chance to step up and redeem ourselves. And maybe we can redeem my husband too."

"I'm not running any charity, lady."

Charity. That was it! Olivia thought about the photos of the Syrian refugees and of the nuns and orphans whose faces filled her dreams. "I'll send the bank account information to you, and you get me everything you can on that account. I want to know how it operated, how involved my husband was, and what he did with the funds. Maybe we can do a little good in the world with that money. And don't let a word of this leak to the press, because as much as I'd hate to play lowball again, if Hudson Bauer's name is compromised in any way, I'll tell the FBI about that hundred spot you used to bribe one of his employees. I imagine that information could place your license in jeopardy. So be a hero, Mr. Brewster. You'll have my email in the hour."

Olivia ended the call, but Susan's pained reaction to it continued. She stared out the basement walkout's sliding doors, looking much as she had that day in Olivia's hospital room.

"None of that sounded like the Jeff I knew."

Olivia was reeling herself and had little comfort to offer. "Maybe we're missing something."

Susan turned and brightened. "Of course. We must be."

Prickles rose on Olivia's arms. She could think of no good explanation that wouldn't build up what could be false hope.

Susan grabbed her coat and headed for the door. "A few of Jeff's college friends came to the funeral or sent cards. I'm going to contact them. Maybe they know something that will explain all this."

"Okay." Olivia heard the doubt in her own voice. She didn't believe Susan would find a happy explanation for Jeff's behavior, but neither could she abide any further discussion of the topic today.

"I'll be in touch," said Susan, as she slipped past the door. Olivia wondered if she'd ever see her again.

CHAPTER TWENTY-ONE

C louds and rain filled most Portland forecasts from October to the year's end. It seemed a fitting prelude to Olivia's feeling about the upcoming holidays. Thanksgiving in Maryland with her mother and Peter Thibodeaux proved to be an unexpected delight. Peter's endless stories about his Cajun boyhood and misspent youth flimflamming tourists in New Orleans left Olivia in stitches. She completely understood why her mother adored the now successful plumbing contractor, and to her surprise, she teared up when it was time to leave them both.

Christmas was spent at Laurel's playing with little Joey. Olivia's thoughts frequently drifted to the baby she had carried so briefly and her January due date. She could no longer picture herself with Jeff and a child, but an ache and emptiness remained.

Hudson sent a package from Africa, where he and his parents were spending the holidays. Inside was a delicate, hand-loomed tablecloth and a beautiful woven basket adorned with a hand-painted elephant. The cover of the card was a sketched Nativity, and inside was a note.

The nuns at the Mother Thomasine's convent make and sell items like these to support themselves and the orphans they teach at their school. Their business is doing well, thanks in great part to your beautiful work on the microbusiness projects. I hope you get to see some of these places and the people you've helped. Thanks also for your support on Sweet Water. You're making a difference.
I hope your Christmas was merry and bright.
Hudson

She debated whether or not Hudson sent gifts to every employee, or if this was his way of reaching out to her, of keeping the door of hope ajar in case they tried again to get it right. She had been so wrong on every point with this good man. She had even picked up the phone a dozen times to admit that very truth, that she now understood her marriage was based on a trick, and that Hudson had given them Arena Corp. But how could she excuse her lack of faith in Hudson?

That question haunted her as she boarded a plane for three days of meetings with Ethan in New York. And, it continued to distract her as she and Ethan designed the brochure to calm the Sweet Water investors—the global committee nervously awaited the most recent set of test results of the revolutionary, but underperforming, solar-powered micro-pump required to make Hudson's dream of Sweet Water possible.

"You seem stuck," said Ethan, as he clicked to open a

folder of photos on his desktop. "Maybe these new photos will ignite that McAllister magic."

She didn't feel like a McAllister anymore.

Especially once images of Hudson appeared on the screen —kneeling by a mud-cracked riverbed, splashing dark-skinned children with water gushing from a hand pump, or sitting cross-legged in a circle with men dressed in tribal colors. She noticed something disturbing.

"He looks—"

"Thin? Sad? Terrible? He hardly spends a week a month in the office anymore. He's practically based in Africa. He's there now. Sweet Water has become his obsession."

"What happened?"

"I thought you might know."

Olivia's heart stopped beating for a moment. "Me? Why me?"

"I thought he might have said something to you. You're clearly important to him. I've watched Hudson's reaction whenever your name is mentioned in a meeting, and I've seen how your eyes keep drifting to his office door. You seem worried about him, too."

"I am … I …" Her phone buzzed with a call from Susan, the women's first contact since October. Olivia excused herself and slipped into the hall to answer.

"Susan, I'm glad you called."

"I'm sorry I haven't been in touch. Are you in your apartment? I have something I need to show you."

There was a tremble in her voice that set Olivia's nerves on edge. "I'm on a business trip. I'll be home on the fifth."

"All right. I'll meet you at your place at ten on Friday. Okay?"

"What's going on, Susan? Just tell me."

"I can't explain it properly. You need to see this. I think you'll feel better about things when you do."

THE WOMAN OLIVIA found standing in her doorway barely resembled Susan. Her jeans and T-shirt were rumpled and grease-spotted, and her hair and eyes looked as if she had just come straight from her bed. She had an iPad in her hands.

"Are you all right?" She hurriedly drew Susan inside and to a kitchen chair.

"I'm fine. I haven't really slept or gone to work since I called you."

"You're scaring me. What's going on?"

"I told you I was going to reach out to Jeff's college teammates to see if he ever told them anything about Arena Corp."

"I remember."

"Well, I've been keeping in touch with one of them. A guy named Walt. He was actually at your wedding ceremony and reception."

Olivia's face blushed hot at the mention of that day. "And?"

"He mentioned something about Jeff's YouTube channel, so I searched for it, and I found it. It was password protected, but I figured it out, and I've been sitting in front of it ever since, just watching clip after stupid clip of Jeff." She started to cry. "But amongst all the juvenile college stuff, he also kept a video journal where he recorded personal messages. Three of them were directly to you … clips he planned to send you, but, for one reason or another, never did. You're going to want to hear these." She booted up the tablet as Olivia held her breath and slipped down into the chair beside her.

"He was drunk when he recorded the first one. The picture is grainy, but you can make out the words. As hard as it's going to be to hear, I think it will help us all understand Jeff."

Susan typed in the search bar, bringing up a YouTube page. The header displayed several captured images of Jeff and friends, but a bleary-eyed image of Jeff filled the rest of the screen. He was wet, as if he'd just taken a shower. A white terry robe hung loose and open, revealing Jeff's damp, bare chest. Wet hair framed his distressed face in brown ringlets, giving him a lost, childlike essence. Olivia saw him as she remembered him before their marriage. Before the deceit. She reached a hand toward the screen, wishing they could connect.

She began to tremble as she read the logo on the robe and viewed the elegant amenities in the bathroom. She recognized the location as the hotel room where they spent their wedding night. Her mind flashed back to the morning after their marriage, when Jeff exited the bathroom with a haunted expression on his face. He had been crying, but when she went to comfort him, he refused her kindness and told her to pack.

She clicked the play button, and Jeff's slurred voice filled the silence.

"Olivia." His head dropped into his hands. "I'm so sorry." She heard muffled moans and then his head lifted again. "If you're seeing this, it means I left. I didn't mean for this to get so far." His face twisted as he fought to control his emotions. "I didn't want Hudson's handout. I just wanted him to admit that what I contributed mattered." He grew more animated. "I thought he took off without me, as if I was nothing to him or the company. Just extra baggage." His finger pointed forward as if punctuating the next statement. "So I headed to the bar and turned off my phone. I swear I didn't get any of his messages."

"Stop," said Olivia. "I don't understand."

Susan paused the clip. "You have to listen to all of the clips to understand. Jeff lied when he told you the Arena Corp meeting had been postponed. Hudson must have taken off early in the morning for some reason, and Jeff assumed he had left for the meeting without him. He felt neglected and angry, so he started drinking and turned off his phone. That's why he missed Hudson's calls and texts and the real departure time, and why Hudson ended up pitching the Arena Corp deal himself. Sit back down. It will all make sense in a minute."

As Olivia sat, Susan resumed the video.

"I told you Hudson was pulling away from us. That he was tossing us aside. I was afraid for me, but I knew he would never bail on you. He was going to propose to you. He was going to have it all—success, wealth, the beautiful wife who supported him." Jeff groaned. "Hudson was always smart, Olivia, but you … you made him believe in himself. That's why you're special." Tears rolled down his face. "So different from the girls I dated. I thought if you could do that for Hudson, maybe you could do that for me too. I needed someone in my corner so badly. I needed you. But I had a very short window to win you over, so I borrowed from Hudson's playbook, and I managed to make you believe you loved me the way I was falling in love with you."

A soft gasp escaped on Olivia's next breath. "Stop the

clip." She shivered and wrapped her arms around herself like a shield. "He did love me?"

Susan placed her hand on Olivia's back. "Yes. That's what I wanted you to hear. What he did was wrong, terribly wrong, but he did love you, Olivia."

She hit "play," and the video continued. "I should never have agreed to a round of drinks at that bar. Our wedding celebration turned into a victory party about me taking what Hudson loved most. I expected you to turn and run any minute, but you didn't." Confusion filled his face. "You stayed. I thought maybe you really did love me." He hung his head and shook it. "But I got so drunk that I forgot the exit strategy." He quieted as his hands covered his head like a helmet.

His head shook as he said, "I swear I was going to tell you the truth. All of it. I was going to tell you that two men loved you—me and Hudson—and let you choose. I thought if I had time alone with you, you might see what I could be, and you might love me the way you loved him. If you chose Hudson, I'd take you home, and we'd annul it all the next day. But I got so messed up."

Jeff bent over and wrapped his arms around his head again, rocking and groaning. When he stood, his eyes glanced down, avoiding the camera. Olivia could barely pull her eyes from the tortured face before her, but neither could she sit. Her body felt like gelatin.

"You were just too kind, Olivia. Too protective. You got us to that hotel, and there you were. So beautiful. So innocent. So loving." He closed his eyes. "I got lost in you."

"Please," cried Olivia, "no more." Her hands came up, shielding her face.

Susan stood beside her. "I can only imagine what you're feeling. I'm just his sister, but the biggest hurt these past six months has come from thinking I never really knew my own brother. That he was Jekyll and Hyde. Now I know that he was a good man who made an unspeakable mistake, and who spent the rest of his life trying to fix it. Please, Olivia. Sit back down and at least finish this clip. I promise, you'll feel your own guilt wash away."

Olivia wondered if she were having a heart attack. Somehow, in that moment, the thought of dying right then didn't frighten her, at least not as much as the regret of knowing what she and Jeff had squandered.

The clip began again, but Jeff was subdued in body and mind.

"When I woke up and saw you there, I remembered everything, and I wanted to die. I've been hiding here in the bathroom, but no matter how many times I've showered, I still feel like dirt. Like a monster. I took everything from you, and I have nothing to offer." He sniffed and rubbed a sleeve across his nose.

"You should be with Hudson." He looked into the camera, straight into her eyes. "I know what I need to do. I'm going to make this as right as I can. I promise. After I rush you back to Hudson, I'll send you this link, and then I'll slip away. I don't know where, but I won't interfere in your life again." His head bent forward, and Olivia killed the feed.

"No more. I know the rest." She slumped into her chair. "Jeff took me back to the apartment, but Hudson had already heard about the wedding, and he was gone."

"That's why Jeff decided to stay and try to be the husband you deserved, but his guilt prevented him from being that man. He made other videos when he thought he'd found the strength to leave. He knew you'd be all right. In one of the clips he says, 'Hudson made sure of that.' I figured it was a reference to Arena Corp."

The words were just white noise to Olivia.

Susan closed the cover on the iPad, but neither woman spoke for several moments.

"He was more resolute in the message made last June, weeks before the accident. Please listen to that clip some time. He thanked you for trying so hard to love a man whose choices left him unable to love himself." Susan touched Olivia's arm. "He also apologized for denying you a family. The thought of that responsibility crushed him, so he pushed you away, hoping you'd leave and find a good man, but you wouldn't go."

Olivia wiped at her eyes. "If I had just known that he cared about me, maybe we could have been happy."

"I think the scars were too deep for both of you at that point. My brother was a proud man. He hated failure of any kind. He knew how much our family loved him, but he chose to avoid us rather than risk having us think he failed."

"He owned a small business. Why couldn't that be enough?"

"We both know he was chasing Hudson's success. I think he hid that money in Switzerland so he wouldn't be tempted to use it. He said he only used it once, and he knew you'd approve of his decision. That's really the essence of Jeff's legacy. He wanted so much to make you proud of him, to succeed on his own, and to leave a positive mark on the world. In the end, he decided that the best thing to do was to leave and end the emotional hemorrhage between you two.

The last video explains his plan to take off the day after the picnic."

"He was going to invest in Ben Ashburn's building project."

"Yes. He planned to take some of the funds and leave you the rest with instructions on how to access the Swiss account. You would have been comfortable for the rest of your life."

Susan packed up her tablet and stood. "I sent you the video links in case you want to view them. I think you should." She bit her upper lip. "I miss him, Olivia, but I think that's a good thing. My brother wasn't a monster. Just a selfish, proud man."

She walked to the door and pivoted. "Jeff is the one who failed your marriage. Not you. But I'm going to repeat the advice I gave you in the hospital. Your life is yours from here on out. So are your choices and the responsibilities that go with them. Jeff hijacked your chance to be with Hudson, but it's your decision whether that separation becomes an end or just an eight-year delay. Hudson still loves you. You clearly love him as well. Go to him. Do it for yourself, for Hudson, and for Jeff."

CHAPTER TWENTY-TWO

J eff knew I loved Hudson. He knew Hudson was set to propose. These two facts turned in Olivia's mind like tumblers in a lock, freeing her from the guilt she bore over her marriage. Knowing that Jeff also loved her—that he hadn't just duped her—eased the suffocating self-doubt that had crippled her for so long. Even so, grief struck her afresh as video images of Jeff's twisted mouth and downcast eyes haunted her, and his pained voice disrupted her sleep.

She was lying in bed one morning after a restless sleep when her phone buzzed with two incoming texts and an attachment from Larry Brewster. The first text read,

-Does this ring any bells?

She downloaded the attachment—a bank image indicating the transfer of eleven million dollars to a nonprofit called "The Pioneer Group." Olivia remembered that the name of the experimental school Susan worked for was "The Pioneer School," and it came with an eleven-million-dollar price tag. Her eyes glistened at the realization that Jeff's one withdrawal from the Swiss account had been to fund the school's construction. He was the benefactor.

Then she read this:

Seven million dollars remains. One million in Jeff's name, and six in yours. Mailing the particulars, including my fee. This concludes our agreement.

She stared at the information for several minutes, allowing the news to sink in. Jeff had tried to make restitution. Again, he had done it without her. They never got anything right.

She called Susan and shared the information. After a joint cry, she hung up the phone and pulled the videos up again. After a few more days of intermittent replays, she said her final goodbye to Jeff, deleted the links, and looked forward.

She suddenly missed her mother and stepfather, and she was no longer afraid to admit that thoughts of Hudson were never far. Her emotional development still felt arrested. She needed more time to feel whole and healthy, but she was ready to go east and begin taking back her life, so she sent Ethan a text, hinting that she would be willing to move to New York.

Ethan's reply came at light speed. "Yes!"

A real estate agent found her a one-bedroom apartment on trendy Roosevelt Island with a February first move-in date. At three thousand dollars a month, she could still manage without touching the Arena Corp money. The thought of having a place of her own changed something in her. She finally felt whole, and a week later, she packed her things, hugged the Ashburns one by one, and headed east.

Her interest in the work was real, but she couldn't deny that her real intent was to have opportunities to see Hudson, to gauge if their already strained relationship had sustained over the ensuing months since that unplanned and unforgettable kiss.

She took a few days' leave to unpack and decided to settle into her office space before going back on the company clock. Ethan greeted her with a wowed expression and a quick hug on her first day in the office.

"Your arrival couldn't have been timed better! I'm about to address a conference of the investors for the microbusiness programs. They've gathered for their annual review."

Despite her protests, he guided her through the back door of a dark conference room where a videotape was playing. As the pair took the remaining two seats, images of dark-skinned nuns in white and blue habits standing before a whiteboard filled the screen. Dozens of dark-skinned children bearing bright smiles sat on a dirt floor, staring up at the letters and words written on the board. The presenter, a woman with a British accent, stopped the media from time to time to explain the video tour of this Catholic convent in the Ivory Coast of West Africa.

"The sisters are a perfect model of what these microbusinesses can become with a little assistance. Besides the bakery, there are homegrown vegetables and fruit and a flock of chickens they began raising last year. Mother Thomasine has encouraged other entrepreneurial plans, and they are now selling eggs and manufacturing candles, medical soap, syrup, and jelly, all of which they sell to support themselves and the needs of local orphans. Their goal is to build a proper orphanage and school inside a concrete wall to protect the orphans from being conscripted by local rebels. Each influx of cash or goods draws these groups' attention and endangers the sisters, so helping the nuns earn the money themselves through our microbusiness ventures has proven to be the safest and most effective plan of support."

Murmurs floated up from the darkened room. It was the first time she had heard about the rebels' threat to the school and convent. Olivia couldn't imagine such danger threatening those joyful faces. The lights came on, and she blinked to adjust her eyes.

The presenter continued. "Your packets contain a list of the twenty American ventures we've also selected for funding. Ethan Machowicz and his team prepared a dossier on each. Ethan, I saw you slip in. Would you like to say a few words?"

Ethan stood beside Olivia. "No, you've covered it beautifully, Arianna. Since all the investors are here, I want to introduce Olivia McAllister. She helped with the Syrian projects, and she's the lead on the American ventures."

Olivia blushed and stood at Ethan's behest. She turned her head to acknowledge each welcoming voice and found herself staring straight into Hudson's onyx eyes. She hadn't seen him in a suit since graduation. At first glance, all she saw was his commanding professional presence, a stark contrast to their last meeting when he arrived exhausted and bedraggled to rescue her. When he told her that he loved her.

There was more about him that caught her attention. Creases and worry showed around his eyes, and he looked as if he had aged years in mere months. They held their gaze for a moment too long before Olivia felt conspicuous. Hudson coughed and stood. "Thank you, Ethan. And thank you, Ms.

McAllister." He picked up a folder from the conference table. "Very good work."

Her tongue felt thick in her mouth. "Thank you," she managed to eke out before she again nodded to the guests. "I look forward to helping in any way I can."

She wanted to murder Ethan, who guided her out the way they entered amidst the exit of the committee.

"You set me up! You knew Hudson was in there."

"Why are you so alarmed?" He leaned in close. "Does he look that bad to you?"

Olivia reined in her indignation as she remembered that to Ethan, she and Hudson were merely old college friends. "He looks exhausted." She looked back in the direction of the room.

"Sweet Water is in big trouble. The rebels are uprising again, threatening anyone who tries to release their hold on the region. Hudson is a threat to them."

"So Hudson is also in danger."

Ethan glanced over her shoulder and coughed, resuming his conversation in a louder voice. "You'll need to update your address. Personnel is two floors down. Go update your information, then check in with my secretary. She'll show you to your office space."

Ethan peeled off, leaving Olivia confused. She moved numbly toward the elevators when she heard a voice from behind. "Liv?"

Now she understood Ethan's quick exit.

Her lips quivered as she turned. She knew better than to try to speak. Hudson came to her, stopping several feet away, his unsteady smile under constant adjustment. "It's good to see you. How long are you in town?"

"For a year at least." Her lips quivered as they formed a forced smile. "I've got a lease on a place on Roosevelt Island."

Hudson's face brightened, and for a moment, Liv saw the return of the young man she once knew. "You moved here? To New York?"

"Yes. Ethan said—"

His smile dimmed to a business-only politeness. Awkwardly, he moved to her, nodding, extending his hand, taking hers, and covering it within his own. "Of course. Ethan asked you. I'm sure he's very happy you accepted his offer."

"No," she said urgently. "I mean … yes, Ethan asked me weeks ago, but that's not why I came. I didn't move here for Ethan or for work. Telecommuting was working fine."

His head cocked slightly to the side. "Then what changed your mind?"

"You. I … I w-wanted to apologize for that last—"

He released her hand and shook his head. His voice lowered to a husky whisper. "There's no need for you to apologize. I shouldn't have pressed you. It won't happen again." He took a step away.

"Wait. So much has happened in the past few months. I moved here to …" Her frustration muddled her thoughts. "Could we possibly talk?"

His face, flush with wonder one moment, quickly shifted to disappointment. "I'm leaving for the helipad right now." Worry etched deep lines in his brow. "It's my parents."

She closed the small gap between them and took hold of his arms before remembering that this man was the head of the corporation, and she was an employee. She stepped back and asked, "What's wrong? How are they?" The news explained the changes she saw in him.

"They're frightened, but otherwise all right." His eyes rolled heavenward. "A rebel band roughed Dad up and threw a stick of dynamite down the shaft of the well he was drilling in Ghana. They issued a warning this time, but they threatened my parents' lives if Dad drills another well."

"Why? Oh, Hudson, I'm so sorry."

Hudson's face melted as his name rolled from her lips. "Water frees people. They can move where they want, grow crops, start businesses, and enjoy previously unimaginable possibilities, and that's the last thing these rebels want."

Determination steeled his expression. "The final tests on the solar battery and pump are critical. If we can power these micro-pumps with the sun, families will be able to poke a tube into a dry riverbed and pull water from the sand." His hand formed a fist. "And if we distribute them widely enough, the rebels will never be able to use water as a weapon again." He closed his eyes and slumped into one hip. "I'm sorry. I'll get off my soapbox now."

"Wait." Worry replaced the warmth seeing him had brought her. "Won't they try to stop you, too?"

"They've threatened as much, so we're moving the tests to a safer place—the Ivory Coast. I have friends there, and a security detail. It's not a typical drought zone, but they're having a dry year, so we'll find dry riverbeds there for the test." He fidgeted, and his eyes kept glancing at his watch. "I'm sorry. I just need to get my parents home. But I really—"

"You need to go. Of course."

His face slackened as he took a slow breath. "I'm sorry. I have a minute. Please … tell me what you wanted to say."

She couldn't adequately focus the myriad feelings swirling

inside her. She knew her joy at seeing him was fully reciprocated, but now he was leaving. Again. Into danger. "It'll keep."

Relief visibly washed over him. "I'm very glad you're here." He gently took her hands. "You can't know how glad I am to see you. I'll get in touch as soon as I'm able. Okay?"

She felt her eyes begin to well as Hudson drew close enough for a momentary embrace.

"Please give your parents my love." She bit her lip. "And please stay safe." Then she turned and headed for the elevators. "Because I love you, Hudson Bauer," she said, when no one but she could hear.

CHAPTER TWENTY-THREE

B rief texts from Hudson appeared on her phone over the next few days.

-Glad to have you in New York. Would love to show you around the city. Mom and Dad are on a plane for Portland. Breathing easier now.

Things here are a mess now. The rebels are even threatening the tribal leaders if they so much as talk to me. They found a local tough guy named Safdar to frighten them. I need to stay here to bolster their confidence. If I lose them, I lose Sweet Water.

-I would love for you to see Africa.

Fear struck her as she read of the rebels' new threats. She knew Hudson risked his own safety for the causes he loved, and she knew he would place himself in danger for Sweet Water. And some rebel named Safdar wanted to stop him. Why hadn't she told him she loved him?

A memo on the dilemmas with the Sweet Water project crossed her email, underscoring Hudson's texts. The tribal leaders' will to support the project was waning as fears mounted over rebel retaliations. As a result, the date of the pump test was moved up substantially. She wanted so much to be there.

She pulled up the folder of photos of Hudson with the children. One photo pictured Hudson watching a nun from Mother Thomasine's convent as she wrote the alphabet on a whiteboard, poised before rows of eager, happy children. All of them were rebel targets. Olivia wanted to do something to help each of them, but she felt powerless from so far away. So far away. Then she would fix that. But, she'd need help from Alejandra, the gatekeeper to Hudson's world, who gave Olivia the death stare every time she even darkened the executive level hall.

Alejandra's elegant shoulders squared as Olivia walked towards her intimidating post.

"Hello, Mrs. McAllister."

"Hello. I just thought we should get to know each other, since we'll be colleagues."

Alejandra placed her arms on the desktop, folded her hands, and leaned toward Olivia. "Oh, I know you already. You're the person Hudson went to Mexico to forget."

The news hit Olivia like a lightning strike, splaying her open like so much dead wood. She was the reason Hudson fled Seattle. Was she also the reason he abandoned grad school for Mexico? With Pepper?

The stone coldness of Alejandra's voice turned to gravel. "You didn't know?"

Olivia faltered for several seconds as she considered the

depths of the despair into which her impulsive marriage had driven Hudson. Her hands shook and she interlocked them to hide her reaction. "Pepper told me he went there after a heartbreak. I suspected it was my marriage, but she wouldn't confirm the timing or say as much. But I know you're the woman who saved him and Pepper." She met Alejandra's eyes. "I know you love him and want to protect him, so one thing we can agree on is that we both care about Hudson."

"Easy words," Alejandra hissed back. "For how long? This week? Two weeks? Until loving Hudson proves inconvenient again?"

The barb struck even more painfully, because Olivia knew this was a good woman that Hudson dearly loved. "You don't like me. I get that, but let me tell you respectfully that you don't have all the facts. Neither does Hudson, nor did I until a few months ago. That's why I've waited until now to come to New York. Until I was sure I had dealt with all the hurt and betrayal of the past."

"And you think you have?"

"Yes."

"Do you know that you are his Achilles heel? His Kryptonite, so to speak? This man's word is his bond, unless you need him more, in which case he drops meetings, flies across continents, and allows his global influence to dim in a world that needs men like him to shine. That's the influence you have on him. Do you love him enough, and in a way that will help Hudson be the man he wants to be?"

Olivia's eyes held Alejandra's like a tractor beam as she considered what the woman was implying about the cost of Hudson's love for her. She could either be an asset or a stumbling block. To be an asset to him, she would have to accept that Hudson would never fully be hers in the traditional family way. They would never have a nine-to-five, dinner-at-six sort of life. She couldn't expect that she or any future children would ever be able to count on him to be there at a specific moment or event if a cause or a problem needed him, because if she protested, he would answer, and projects would remain merely plans, and hopes would go unanswered. It was a daunting thought.

And then she remembered something Jeff said in the video. Hudson was always smart, but you, Olivia, you made him believe in himself.

Alejandra sat back and nodded appreciatively at Olivia. "I appreciate that you understand why—"

"Yes." Olivia lifted her head and set her eyes on Alejandra's. "Yes, I do think I love him in a way that will help him be that light. Because I was there in the beginning. Me. Hudson and I dreamed the first dream together." She stood and held her hands outward. "These hands helped him make it come true. We were barely more than children when circumstances separated our paths, but I believe that we were always meant to be together, and I'm not going anywhere."

A smile spread across Alejandra's lips. "I finally meet the woman Hudson described."

Nearly breathless with relief, Olivia leaned close. "I need to get to the Ivory Coast."

The woman's head shook with a firm no. "You cannot go to the Sweet Water site. It's too dangerous. The company pilots are ex-military because they are also part of the needed security."

"I love Hudson, and I'm going to be with him even if I have to book my own flight."

Long moments passed before Alejandra stood and began writing on the back of a business card. "We have a plane leaving for the Ivory Coast in three hours to carry the pump and supplies for the test." She handed the card to Olivia. "Do you have a passport?"

Olivia was grateful she had applied for one months ago when Ethan scheduled her for the canceled trip to Turkey. "Yes."

"Good. Here's the hangar number. Go home and pack some light work clothes. The temperatures in the inland areas exceed one hundred degrees this time of year. I'll call our pilot and tell him to wait for you."

"What about Ethan?"

"I'll square things with Ethan. Now go. Go!"

Olivia remembered her idea. "I'd like to take something to Mother Thomasine's orphans."

"Something small?"

Olivia gestured to illustrate one electronic tablet's size.

"As long as it's all right with the pilot."

She was determined to make it all right with the pilot. She wanted to throw the whole of the Arena Corp money into a fund for the orphanage, but she knew if money were the answer, Hudson would have fully funded the school long ago. Then she remembered Arianna's presentation and her warning that less was safer than more for the nuns because small gifts were less likely to draw the rebels' attention. She called a big box store, ordering a modest number, twelve electronic tablets, for the children's classroom.

"That would be a factory case," said the ecstatic commissioned sales rep.

"I'm delivering them to a school in the Ivory Coast, so can

you also prepare whatever documentation I need for customs? And there's a two-hundred-dollar tip if you deliver them to hangar three at Teterboro Airport by two o'clock."

With that task handled, the impact of her pending trip to Africa hit her. What would Hudson think? Each time her nerves weakened her will, she remembered that Hudson had flown across the world for her. Surely he would understand her own gesture of commitment.

She asked the taxi driver to keep the meter running while she packed and changed into jeans and layered tops she could shed once she left New York's cold. The driver weaved and dodged through the winter slush on the ride to JFK. An unmarked Gulfstream G4 waited on the tarmac in front of hangar three. Two men, one tall African-American and another, shorter man who Olivia assumed were the pilots, were performing a pre-flight check as the taxi pulled up. Olivia paid the driver, and as she exited the cab, the taller pilot extended his hand. "Michael Lath at your service," he said, with a beautiful African accent tinged with French.

"Thank you for taking me," said Olivia, as she paid the driver who unloaded her things.

"We thank you," said the other pilot, in noticeably Australian tones. He offered his hand and said, "Buddy McIntlock. We were scheduled to fly an old cargo plane, but Alejandra upgraded us. I suppose she didn't want two former military pilots flopping you around in the back for eight hours. Now, let's get your things loaded, shall we?"

Before Olivia answered, Michael pointed to the carton of tablets. "Alejandra gave me the pump and piping. She didn't mention any other cargo."

"It's a last-minute addition. Can you fit it in?"

"May I see the paperwork?" She handed him the customs documents, and his brow wrinkled as he studied them. "Our final destination is Gagnoa, but we can't land this jet on the short dirt runways there, so we must transfer to a small Cessna in the morning. It will be a tight fit with that carton." He shook his head. "And it will draw attention." Lines formed on his tight brow. "Please board now while I file my flight plan."

Buddy welcomed her into the luxurious cabin of the Gulfstream and settled her into a buttery soft leather seat fit for a king or a president. "Is this the company's jet?" she asked, as she squeezed the soft armrests and reclined. "I didn't see the Bauer Group logo on the side."

Buddy smiled at her. "It's one Mr. Bauer uses to fly important guests when we need to arrive—how shall I put this—incognito. I'll go load your carton now."

Olivia wondered if the rebels were the reason they needed to be covert. The question plagued her through takeoff, until the rocking rhythm of the Gulfstream lulled her to sleep. When she awoke, she saw nothing but starlight ahead and a vast unforgiving ocean below, signaling that they were still over the Atlantic.

She walked up the aisle to the open cockpit door. Buddy turned and smiled. "Just a few more hours now."

"When did Hudson Bauer decide to send that case of tablets?" Michael asked.

Olivia sensed the worry in his voice. "He didn't. I asked Alejandra if I could bring something for the children, and she said it would be all right if it was small and okayed by you."

Michael's worried gaze shifted to Buddy. "I believe she meant small like a lollipop."

Olivia's arms prickled. "Are these tablets going to cause problems?"

"We will not know until we reach Gagnoa."

Michael's final comment hung like a sword over the rest of the flight. Olivia was relieved when things appeared to go smoothly after landing in Bouaké, Ivory Coast. After routine checks of papers and cargo, the three left the airport to spend the night in a hotel, returning at first light to load their luggage and cargo into a Cessna. Three armed men watched them near the hangar.

Olivia hurried up to Michael who was checking the plane. "Those men are carrying guns. Do you think they're with Safdar?"

"Or someone loyal to him. Nothing passes through these airports without his knowledge."

"Maybe we should just dump the tablets here. Let them have them."

"That won't help us now. The rebels in Gagnoa are likely expecting them to arrive there. This plane and each of us will be searched whether we have them or not."

Hudson's conversation about the warning the rebels gave his father echoed in her mind as a chill zipped up her spine. "If they search us, they might find the pump."

The normally affable Buddy scowled. "We'd best get on our way as soon as possible."

The relief of takeoff and the peaceful hour-long hop to Gagnoa ended in tension when the satellite phone rang in the cockpit as they prepared to land. Buddy answered the call while Michael landed the plane, leaving a wild plume of dust billowing behind.

Olivia couldn't hear the phone conversation, but she read

Buddy's lips as he leaned near Michael, his worry evident. "Hudson is coming in person to get the pump. He's almost here."

The muscles along Michael's jaw tensed as he looked toward the local crowd, where several armed men dressed in camo pants and sleeveless shirts began moving toward the taxiing Cessna. Once again, the rebels' warning replayed in Olivia's mind. What had Hudson said?

Water frees people. That's the last things these rebels want …

She and her misguided decision to bring those tablets had drawn the rebels here, making targets of them and their cargo. Now Hudson would also be in danger, as would the prototype pump. Olivia knew Hudson and the entire Sweet Water project were at risk. Because of her. Because, once again, her judgment had been off.

Her breathing became rapid as the armed men closed the distance to the plane. Olivia forced herself to move past her guilt and think. A quick scan of the terrain reminded her of one of Peter Thibodeaux's stories, giving her an idea. It was hazardous, but it was less risky than the sure danger Hudson would face if he arrived. With her heart pounding, she laid out her plan.

"I caused this danger, but I have an idea. We need to get that pump to Hudson, but we can't let him be seen by the rebels. Safdar has made him a target, so we need to divert their attention long enough to sneak the pump past them. Michael, if you steer this plane near that brush on the right, Buddy can bail out and hide in there. Then, while the plane taxis back to the terminal building, he can get to Hudson and convince him to head for the test site."

Michael kept idling down the runway and away from the airport while Buddy protested.

"And leave you and Michael here to face the rebels alone? No way, ma'am. I'd rather take my chances with the rebels than with Hudson if anything happens to you on our watch."

"Protecting me won't save Hudson or the pump." Buddy grew quiet. The rebels were agitated now and closing fast. With time growing increasingly short, Olivia pressed on. "We just need to convince them that we're here to deliver those tablets and not pump supplies."

"And how do you plan to do that?"

"A little diversion and a scam called the Flimflam. I'll keep them occupied while you get the pump to Hudson."

Buddy's jaw clenched as he dug in on his refusal. Olivia's hands were shaking as she looked to Michael. "You know it's the only way to protect us or Hudson or that pump. This situation is all my fault, but I can do this. I need to do this. Please, trust me."

Michael spent a moment chewing on the side of his mouth before abruptly steering the plane toward the brush, sending the rebels racing across the dirt strip in their direction.

"You can't go along with this!" Buddy argued to Michael.

"She is right. If Safdar wins now ... if he defeats Hudson, the leaders may never have the will to stand up to him again. The rebels will see this fancy American lady as a misguided philanthropist, not a well driller. You go. Keep Hudson away. These are my people. I know what that pump means to them, so I will stay with Olivia and pray that God will smile on each of us."

The exasperation on Buddy's face turned to acceptance as he looked at Olivia. "You're a brave gem of a woman, Liv."

She forced her lips to still their trembling. "Liv? That's what Hudson calls me."

"I know," he said in his thick Australian drawl. "He talks when he sleeps in-flight."

The comment sent Olivia's heart pounding even more. As the plane drew beside the brush, Buddy rolled out the plane's door and into the cover of the brush. Olivia took his seat as Michael turned the plane back toward the airport. Within fifty yards, the sweat-soaked African rebels caught up to the plane with their guns raised, ordering the passengers to deplane.

Michael slowed the Cessna to a halt, and the rebels threw the doors open, shouting in a French dialect as they gestured for them to step out and onto the tarmac. Olivia understood a few words, but the rebels' body language and glaring eyes told her all she needed to know. They were angry and dangerous.

Automatic weapons were brandished with fury as they cursed in French. Michael wisely shook his head and touched his ear, pretending not to understand them. The apparent leader of the four-man group began communicating in English. Now Olivia could follow the conversation and eventually play her part.

"Where is the copilot?" demanded the leader. "There were two men in Bouaké."

"As you can see, he did not complete the last leg of the flight with us."

The youngest rebel tossed a braid over his shoulder and pressed a gun barrel into Michael's cheek while the leader snarled, "You think I am a fool? The fuel for that plane was reserved and purchased a week ago using a Bauer Group credit card. You see? Safdar knows everything that happens. Tell me, what have you brought to my country? Safdar has already warned Hudson Bauer about interfering in our affairs. Where is he?"

Olivia leaned back against the plane on jelly-like legs as she wondered that as well. She willed herself not to glance in the direction from which Hudson would be arriving, silently praying that Buddy reached Hudson in time, and that he'd be successful in stopping him from attempting a rescue.

"Where is Hudson Bauer?" the rebel repeated to Michael with a shake of his automatic weapon. "And what equipment have you brought him?"

Something about the rebel's French dialect reminded Olivia of Peter Thibodeaux, calming her. She needed to pivot the conversation away from Hudson, but how? Crazy or divine inspiration flashed into her mind, telling her to mimic Peter's inflections and Cajun vocabulary, masking her connection to Hudson Bauer.

Willing her quaking legs to still, she pushed away from the plane and faced the rebel leader. "You are correct," she said with Cajun intonations. "The plane was chartered from The Bauer Group, but I bought these tablets. I have the receipt to prove that I am the benefactor."

Confusion and intrigue showed on the man's face, along with suspicion. Olivia increased the ruse. "We will pay you well for your help in transporting our cargo to its destination."

The ludicrous comment and her tones seemed to momentarily baffle the rebels. The dread-headed young man let his gun slip as he stared at her. His accomplices smirked while the leader sneered at Olivia. "You no longer have cargo. It is now the property of the Forces Nouvelles de Côte d'Ivoire. I will see our cargo now!"

Ignoring the rubbery condition of her legs, Olivia stood eye-to-eye with the leader as they moved to the cargo door. She ratcheted up her Cajun performance to distance herself from Hudson and the water project. "Perhaps you have heard of my father—Peter Thibodeaux, of New Orleans? I saw a documentary about a local orphan school. The plane and pilot were chartered so we could bring the children these electronic tablets."

The leader swung his incredulous gaze to each of his men. "They want to help the children!" He laughed in a derisive tone and shoved the gun into Olivia's side. "Open the box!"

HUDSON BAUER'S gut knotted as he caught sight of a man hiding in the scrub growth along the roadside. "Do you see him?" he asked his driver as they slowed.

Hudson recognized the man who ran into the center of the dirt road and waved his arms, but that recognition brought deeper concerns. As the Jeep drew closer, Hudson called out, "Buddy?" He opened the door and jumped from the vehicle. "What are you doing in the middle of the airport road? Where's Michael? Is he all right?"

Buddy slouched and diverted his eyes. "We've run into a bit of trouble, Hud. There were rebels waiting for us at the airport. I was sent to warn you and hand you this." He placed the pump and piping in Hudson's hands before meeting his employer's eyes. "Liv insisted."

Hudson's throat tightened as he dropped the pipes and dug his fingers into Buddy's shoulders. "Liv? Olivia McAllister is back there? And you left her?" He shoved Buddy to the ground and ran back to the Jeep.

Buddy scrambled to his feet and stood in front, creating a barrier. "Think first, Hud!" His Aussie accent was filled with emotion as he shouted above the rumble of the engine. "All you'll accomplish by barging in there is to get yourself and them killed. I had the same initial reaction, but Liv changed my mind. She has a plan, and sadly, something she needs to prove to you. But you would know more about that than I, wouldn't you?"

The steel set of Hudson's limbs and jaw melted into fear as he remembered the conversation preceding their first and only kiss back at the beach house after rescuing her. He had indicted her about her failures and lack of faith in him. Had he pushed her to this?

Nothing he had ever done, nothing he had planned for the future mattered in that moment. Nothing had meaning without Liv, whom he felt powerless to help. Buddy was right. He would only place her in further danger by rushing in. He felt much as he had that day in the hospital when she threw him out and turned him away. "I can't just do nothing." His voice sounded ancient, defeated. "She's everything to me."

Buddy placed his hand on Hudson's shoulder. "You two have a strange way of communicating, because it would seem that's what she's trying to tell you as well."

Without shame, Hudson turned his welling eyes to Buddy.

"Does that surprise you, my friend?" Buddy spoke quietly. "I've known for some time that there was someone special out there named Liv, but since you never spoke of her openly, I figured she was someone lost to you. I don't know why you're not together, but she put your safety, your life, and your dream ahead of her own security. She asked all of us to trust her. I think we should, but you must decide for yourself."

Every nerve in his body was firing. He needed to run, to get to Olivia, but his driver had the only weapon available, and it was a pistol—no match against automatic weapons. And then he got an idea.

OLIVIA'S HANDS were shaking so badly she couldn't release the tape on the carton. The rebel pushed in beside her and produced a knife, which caused her to gasp and shrink back a step.

He laughed. "Did you think I was going to cut you? If I wanted to kill an American, I would have already shot you."

She took some comfort in his comment, knowing she also needed to keep this man from changing his mind. She swallowed to regain her composure. "Who are you?"

His head shot her way. "No names."

Their faces were so close she could feel his spittle sprinkle her cheek, but she dared not wipe it away.

He sliced through the tape and rifled through the box, counting and admiring each tablet he pulled from the carton, even mentioning their model number. When he reached the bottom, he shoved the box to the parched ground and called two of the other rebels by name. "Search every inch of this plane."

His interest in the tablets heartened Olivia, but the rebels were still there brandishing their guns, so she needed to continue the negotiations. "I'll make you a deal. I'll give you half the tablets if you let me have the other half for the orphans."

His bright teeth glowed against his dark skin as he sneered. "I ... keep ... them ... all." Each word was clipped and exaggerated.

The final moment had arrived, and if all went well, Olivia hoped the rebels searching the plane would be told to stop and the four men would take the tablets and leave. Olivia gave the leader a look of resignation and rounded her shoulders. "You win. Please take them as my gift." Her conscience couldn't stop her tongue. "But first, tell me one thing. Why do you fight those who are trying to help your people?"

Eyes that celebrated victory a moment earlier now darkened. His hand came up, jabbing a finger near her face. "You know nothing about my country and people. We are diverse, from many nations, many political ideologies, many religions —Muslim, Christian, those who believe the old ways." He leaned in close and snarled. "Do not presume to know what is best for us."

She held her breath, regretting her words. A few seconds felt like an hour, and then he called to his two companions searching the plane.

"Come. Get Aristide. It's time to go."

Out of the corner of her eye, she saw one of the men in the plane raise a piece of paper and call for the leader. She recognized it as a page from one of the brochures. A sheen of sweat spread over her body as the leader reached through the open hatch to retrieve the document. If he read the word "pump" in the text, she and Michael would be in danger again.

The leader's eyes moved across the page when a siren sounded and a red glow appeared from down the road.

"Des soldat!" growled the leader as he tossed the paper to the ground. "Allez! Allez!"

He and his colleagues filled their arms with tablets, which they juggled on their run to a battered truck parked near the terminal.

During the rebels' chaotic retreat, Michael ran to Olivia, placing his body between her and the rebels.

"Michael, that rebel was about to read the customs manifest. Those soldiers just saved us."

"Not the soldiers," smiled Michael. He pointed toward the light and sound show. "Look."

A Jeep rounded a bend in the road with only one passenger—a driver—but off to the side of the road, in the brush, two men watched the rebels' truck speed away from the light and siren blare. When they stood up, Olivia recognized them immediately. Buddy leapt in the air and cheered while Hudson broke from the cover, heading her way in a dead run.

Breathless and pale with worry, he stopped mere feet from her as his eyes surveyed her condition. Olivia's voice cracked, and without a word, he scooped her into his arms and pressed her close, burying his face in her hair. She heard no words other than the graveled repeat of her name, and the shuddering breaths of relief rushing past her ear.

Olivia returned the embrace, tightening her arms around Hudson, feeling once more that she was made to fit this very man. The enormity of the risk she had taken flooded upon her, and she wet Hudson's shoulders with tears of relief. Hudson pulled back, his mouth still agape, worry still visible in the creases of his face and in his shining eyes. He framed her face in his hands, brushing her hair back. His lips trembled as his thumbs traced along her jaw. "I lost you once. I'd never survive losing you again."

"I'm sorry. I'm so sor—"

"I love you," he muttered in a breathless rush. Further speech was silenced as Hudson's hungry mouth pressed over hers. His pounding heart throbbed against her, its steady rhythm quieting the shaking of her body, replacing it with peace and security. Her arms moved up his back, preventing his escape. This time, her thoughts were consumed with only one man—Hudson Bauer.

The kiss ended, but the need to connect remained. Cheek to cheek, brow to brow, Olivia finally said the words she'd travelled thousands of miles to say. "I love you. I never stopped." His arms reached for her again, and she settled in against him like a second skin. "I have so much to tell you. I know all about Arena Corp and the money. Thank you for always looking out for me."

"Every day. Always."

She pulled back again to meet his love-filled eyes. "I finally put all the pieces together. I found your proposal book. That's what you went back to Portland to get the night—" Her eyes lowered in shame, then rose again, pleading, earnest, to meet Hudson's. "Jeff stole from it that night in the apartment. He said and did all the right things, but it was your words and ideas I fell in love with, not his. He told me you were moving on without us. I should have trusted you, but I let my fears overrule my heart. I'm so sorry. Can you forgive me?"

He kissed her head. "That's all in the past. What you did today ..." His eyes closed and his head shook as if he were reliving a nightmare. When he reopened them, they shone as he stared into hers. "Did I push you to this? Did I make you feel you needed to prove something to me?"

Beads of sweat streaked down Hudson's face, leaving trails along his cheeks. She reached a dirt-stained hand up and pressed it there. "I needed to prove something to myself. There's so much more I need to tell you."

"We have time. All the time in the world."

Hudson pulled her hand away and placed a knee-weakening kiss in her palm that overwhelmed her remaining strength. She slumped into the arm wrapped protectively around her as his lips found hers again in a soft kiss that deepened moment by moment. His hand released hers to rest against the plane as he leaned their bodies back, pressing into the privacy found in the crook between the wing and fuselage. Olivia felt his heart beat against hers, their every breath timed to their salty kisses.

At last, they were as one, as it was always meant to be.

CHAPTER TWENTY-FOUR

The last embers of the previous evening's fire had burned to hot ash, their glow in the gray of dawn casting shadows across Olivia's sleeping face as she rested in Hudson's arms. Lifting his head from the sleeping bag, he gazed down at her and smiled as a new found contentment radiated through him. He pulled her closer, and she rustled as his hand slid down her sleeve to intertwine his fingers with hers. Every inch of him hungered to touch her, to immerse in the wonder her love brought him. But nothing short of the original dream of making her his wife would satisfy. There was time. They would take things slowly. He would follow her lead.

She stirred and opened her eyes. "Good morning."

He welcomed her with a lingering kiss. "This was worth waiting eight years for."

"All I've ever wanted was you. You're the reason I moved to New York."

His face slackened. "That's what you were trying to tell me back at the office that last day. And I ... I rushed away. I'm so sorry."

"No." She pressed her finger over his lips. "You were worried about your parents. I understood. What matters to you, matters to me. That's why I'm here. I want to be with you when your dream comes true."

ONLY SEVEN TRIBAL leaders out of the twelve Hudson had contacted agreed to come to the designated location for the test. They had been collected in two U.N. vehicles with armed guards in each. Olivia was standing by Hudson's side as Michael and Buddy drove up in the lead escort vehicle.

"I have to tell you, mate, I didn't believe it would work."

"What?" asked Liv.

"That slick trick Hud used on those rebels to rescue you. See, they're mercenaries of a sort. They put President Ouattara in power in exchange for twenty thousand dollars each, which they were never paid. Now they're fighting the very government they infiltrated and put in place. Hud banked on the hope they wouldn't want to be arrested and have their fates determined by their former friends in the government."

"And the innocent citizens get caught in the middle," added Michael Lath.

Buddy nodded in agreement. "Lucky for all of us, Hud here had the bullhorn, flares, and siren alarm the foremen use to clear workers from an area before a detonation. He hoped the rebels would think the feds were the on their trail. Smart man! I'll never doubt him again."

Olivia looked into his eyes. "Neither will I."

"We'd be wise to make this quick," warned Michael, as he exited his Jeep. "We were watched as we made our way here."

"Agreed," said Hudson. He squeezed Olivia's hand and smiled. "A kiss for luck?"

Their lips met as the first armored U.N. vehicle arrived, and seven nervous leaders stepped out, scanning the perimeter. Olivia studied Hudson's face and saw the worry tingeing his excitement. "You don't need luck. All four tests have proven successful."

"These men have risked everything on my promises, and we're going into an untested dry riverbed today."

"You're Hudson Bauer. You make miracles happen. I believe in you."

He held her with his eyes, expressing love in that moment with greater impact than any spoken words. "Do you have any idea how grateful I am that you're here?" he whispered, with a final squeeze of her hand.

She blushed as warmth radiated through every limb. "Go greet your guests."

As he stepped toward the convoy's passengers, his hand slipped beyond her reach. She missed his closeness instantly. Her eyes shone as the man who could buy and sell small nations graciously deferred to each of the courageous leaders.

She marveled at how their lives had been cosmically altered by a few miscalculated hours, unspoken words, and misplaced fears. Yet, here they were. Somehow, heaven had righted what fools had made wrong.

His patience and gentleness gave her confidence as they each navigated what was, in truth, their first experiences with love. And this was love, where smiles warmed her as deeply as kisses. Where a gentle touch both satisfied and stirred. As if hearing her heart, he turned and reached a hand back encouraging her to join him and his guests.

The tribal leaders' wary eyes gave way to smiles as they acknowledged Olivia. Hudson graciously led the way while Michael, who would serve as the interpreter, deferred to one particular leader who Olivia assumed was held in greater esteem than the rest. The leaders took their places at the edge of a dried depression that ran through barren land. A few scrubby plants poked through the baked earth, but the elevated banks were the only clues that this was once a thriving riverbed. The barren spot seemed like worthless land, but the presence of Buddy and the armed U.N. security detail proved how crucial this spot was at that moment.

Hudson entered the bed and carefully drove eighteen inches of narrow pipe into the crust. "The pump only works with this experimental solar battery." He paused as Michael translated his words into French and two African dialects for their guests. "This is a prototype, and we are hurrying to manufacture more." Again, he paused for the translations. Then he placed his ear over the top of the pipe to listen. Disappointed, he withdrew the metal pipe and inserted it again a few feet to the left. Again, he listened for what Olivia knew was the change in sound he expected when the pipe hit underground water. The third test site also failed.

Several of the local leaders crested the riverbank, searching the scrub growth yards from Hudson's position. After a few moments, one of them looked up and smiled, calling to Hudson.

"He wants you to try there," Michael translated.

Hudson nodded and offered the pipe to the leader who

pointed at a particular plant, gesturing about the length of its deep taproot. Hudson bowed slightly at the waist and stepped back, asking the man to proceed. After a few moments, the pipe was inserted, and one by one, the leaders listened to the sound within the pipe, and smiled. They then gestured to Hudson, who listened and smiled with equal pleasure.

Olivia clapped and nearly cried with relief. As Hudson attached the lunchbox-sized solar battery and pump assembly to the pipe, Olivia recalled what the rebel had said, that these well-meaning Americans should not assume that they know Africa and her people. Clearly, the leaders proved today that their knowledge could not be underestimated.

Once the pump was secure and the switch turned on, the motor began to rumble. Within a few seconds, brown water spurted from the pump, followed a minute later by clearer water, filling a small bucket from which the men began ladling.

A cheer sounded from one, while others looked on in measured respect. Olivia watched Hudson's reaction as his eyes moved to the last man, the leader held in the greatest regard by his colleagues. Quiet filled the circle as the bucket was passed to him. He drained the ladle before replacing it in the bucket. His lips smacked loudly, and a smile spread across his face as he uttered two short French phrases.

Again, Michael provided the translation. "The water is sweet. The pump is good."

The other Bauer Group men whooped and smacked Hudson on the back. The flow continued until the bucket was filled several times, at which point Hudson stopped the pump to preserve the precious fluid. As Michael continued answering questions, Hudson left the circle of chattering men and set his eyes on Olivia. With arms spread, he scooped her against him and swung her around.

"You did it! Sweet water!" she said. "Your great-grandmother would be so proud of you."

Hudson set her down and brushed her hair back from her face. "She would have loved you."

"Thanks for waiting for me to figure things out."

"You were worth waiting for, however long it took."

Olivia squeezed his hands. "We need to celebrate."

Hudson scanned the barren perimeter and smiled. "We don't have a lot of options out here in the desert." He tightened his arms around her. "What did you have in mind?"

Her eyes shone as she looked directly into his. "There's a book I've been dying to have you read to me."

Several seconds passed, and then a smile brightened his entire face. "You brought it? The P³?"

She nodded. "I kept it when I moved out of the beach house. I think you're going to like the way the story ends."

Hudson's hands cupped her face as he moved within a breath of her. His eyes studied hers as he brushed an almost imperceptible kiss over her lips and whispered, "The sequel should be even better."

Liv nestled into him, claiming the spot nearest his heart. "I couldn't agree more."

– THE END –

ACKNOWLEDGMENTS

Sweet Water was originally written as a volume in Gelato Books' *Destination Billionaires' Romance Series*. My thanks go to Gelato's owner, Christine Dymock, for inviting me to leave my four-hundred-word comfort zone and write my first novella. Now that the DBR series has run its course, *Sweet Water* will become part of a new series I'm launching—*Second Chance Romances*. I hope you'll try the other books in that series. I've included an excerpt from *Awakening Avery* after these acknowledgements.

Many thanks to a patient hubby and family for not getting too frustrated at me when I slip away from a conversation to jot down a thought I dare not forget. Thanks, Tom, for supporting my addiction to the written word, and for understanding that I'm happiest when I've got a good story in the works. Love you, Honey! And many thanks to my children by marriage and birth—Tom and Krista, Adam and Brittany, Amanda and Nick, Josh and Sidney, and to all my cute grandchildren—Tommy, Keira, Christian, Brady, Avery, Desmond, Chase, Wes, Noah and Kenzie, for helping me find beauty and joy in even the simplest moments. I love you all.

Son Adam, daughter-in-law Brittany, and my cute grand-kids—Chase, Noah, and Kenzie—introduced me to the beautiful Oregon coastline. I had *Sweet Water* plotted out by the time we left Short Sands Beach. Thank you guys, for great memories and views that inspired this book.

I'm blessed with a great support squad. I love my critique ladies—Elizabeth Petty Bentley, Sarah Lee, Lisa Swinton, and Lisa Rector, whose feedback and ideas fueled me during this project. Great thanks go to my Willowsport Crew of beta readers: Christine Clark, Mary Beth Cook, Emma Davis, Pam Dove, Diane Ferguson, Shauna Joesten, Laura Lewis, Kathy McQueeny, Khadra Michaelson, Chantal Preuninger, June Nair, Cyndy Packer, Suzann Schonberger, Jennifer Starkey, Norma Wahlquist, Heather Watson. Their feedback was immensely helpful in smoothing out potholes in the story. Thank you, ladies. You are incredible!

Most importantly, I would like to acknowledge two women and the work they do, for inspiring the humanitarian aspects of "Sweet Water."

Hudson refers to the AMAR foundation on page eight of the book. A dear friend introduced me to this foundation a few years ago, and I was privileged to meet the chairwoman of AMAR, Baroness Nicholson of Winterbourne, while assisting at a reception in her honor near Washington D.C. AMAR provides health care and education to families living in war zones or in areas of civil disorder and disruption. Ninety percent of all donations go directly to helping the people AMAR serves. When so many of us feel helpless to make a difference, here is a safe, trustworthy way we can all help. Click https://www.amarfoundation.org/en-us/ to make a donation.

The nuns and orphans mentioned in "Sweet Water" are based on an actual convent in The Ivory Coast of Africa. Another friend, Dr. Melei Lath, introduced me to her sister, Mother Eugenie, the Mother Superior of The Fraternité Monastique Des Soeurs de Jesus-Euchariste. These nuns support themselves and use their earnings to protect and educate orphans left alone as a result of disease and war. Their great hope is that they will someday be in a position to build a proper orphanage where they can protect the children from rebels.

Lastly, I thank you, my readers, for embracing "Sweet Water" and my other novels. You are the reason I write. Thank you for sharing this journey with me.

Please consider joining other avid readers through my VIP Readers" Club at http://www.laurielclewis.com/newsletter. There are contests, raffles, and behind the scenes news. It's a blast! And follow me on social media to get updates on the release of my newest book, a rewrite of a favorite title—*Awakening Avery*. A preview follows. Enjoy!

AWAKENING
Avery

BY AWARD-WINNING AUTHOR
LAURIE LEWIS

A PREVIEW

Logan, Utah, Late February

Avery Elkins Thompson felt as if her world had been placed in a blender and set to "pulverize." Most of the elements of her life were still there. She was still a mother, and a woman, though she no longer felt womanly in the way she once had. Her career was all but over, little more than a collection of dusty bestsellers released five years or more ago. They sat on a shelf along with her other abandoned dreams, her confidence, and her happiness. All "weres" and "nevermores" because Paul was gone. Avery was no longer a wife. She was a widow.

What she also was, she determined, was a student, albeit unwillingly enrolled in a course of study not of her choosing. The first lesson on widowhood was learned during that early July week of tearful hugs, casserole drop-offs, and funeral services. It was the hardest, however, certainly not the last tutorial she'd receive.

Besides love and compassion, she saw something else in

the eyes of her friends and family members. She had become a person to be pitied and feared—every married woman's reminder of their greatest terror, and every squeamish man's reminder of his mortality. Needing time to accept her new reality, she actually felt a measure of relief when the last friend's car finally pulled out and her worried adult children returned to their own lives. The last child out closed the door with a hesitant click, leaving Avery truly alone for the first time in twenty-eight years—since marrying Paul.

She explained her ongoing reclusiveness as creative downtime, pasting on smiles during family visits, at church, and when cornered during her rare forays out. The dowdy, frightened woman she faced in the mirror each morning worried her. When the daily malaise became overwhelming, Avery pulled it together enough to see the doctor to be sure her own heart wasn't failing. Surreally, the thought of dying didn't frighten her, not at first, anyway, until she considered what losing two parents would do to her children. She kept the appointment, but as soon as she knew her heart was fine, the rest of the diagnosis seemed trite.

"You're depressed," the doctor declared.

Ya think? she felt like saying, but she simply closed her eyes and nodded politely as two prescriptions were shoved into her hand. After eight months, her medicated veneer of okay-ness finally cracked.

She smashed the ancient television first.

That wasn't her intention when she fumbled with the remote for ten minutes, trying to find something to occupy her racing mind. And then, the DVR brought up the screen with the list of programs to record—his list, filled with westerns and mysteries and classic comedies. That was all it took.

She hurled the remote across the room, not intending for it to hit the center of the screen, but it did.

There was something surprisingly cathartic about the sound. The cracking glass and sprinkling shards seemed familiar to her, empty echoes, like those of her long-denied heart, which similarly broke into a thousand pieces each morning she awoke in an empty bed or entered the bathroom where only one toothbrush hung in the holder. Pent-up emotions rushed out like a primal scream, and as if possessed, Avery lashed out at the other instruments of torture Paul had left behind—the decades-old VCR that ate a precious video-tape of their early years together, and the vacuum cleaner that gobbled one of his anniversary cuff links. The crime required the ultimate penance, complete disassembly. Then, soaked with tears, Avery went after the real enemy.

She clicked the mouse on the computer in Paul's study and brought up folders filled with letters and love notes sent from across the globe. She read each one, lamenting over the dates in the headers. The last email had been written on his last day, almost eight months earlier, at an airport gate in Chicago. Avery shut her eyes but the words from his letters and notes came anyway, memorized words read a hundred times over, filled with private jokes and tender expressions of long-distance longings. She could barely breathe. A final look at an image pasted into one of the letters sent her over the edge, and she swept the entire computer system onto the floor. As the printer slid off the desk, she saw herself reverting to the crisis-driven, fists-at-the-ready person she was before Paul, and she slumped over the keyboard, crying as pages of B's swept across the screen.

The following day was more productive.

An hour's shopping, a home installation visit, and $3,327.98 later, all was nearly as good as new. All except for the gouge in the wooden floor, where the old TV landed, and the remains of a few mangled USB cords. Her children and her son-in-law arrived the next day to help their mother survive her first wedding anniversary as a widow.

"The place looks great, Mom," Wes gushed with surprise. "Cool flat screen. I'm glad you've finally done something for yourself."

The phrase "You have no idea" rattled around in her mind, but Avery steeled her will and smiled innocently. "Thank you, Wes," she said, never missing a beat as she whipped cream for pie, while offering her cheek to receive a kiss from her unmarried, twenty-six-year-old son.

The buzzer went off on the oven, and Avery wiped her hands so she could retrieve the rolls.

"I'll get them. You sit down," daughter Jamie insisted, taking hold of her mother's shoulders and leading her to a chair. "You look tired."

The concern in Jamie's voice brought a protective Luke rushing into the kitchen. "Mom is tired?"

Avery noted the worry-driven, slower-tempo, higher-pitched, as-if-they-were-talking-to-a-child intonation that annoyingly rose even higher at the end of each phrase, particularly when it included the word "Mom." It was different with Luke. Only nineteen and quiet by nature, he tended to express his emotions with volume. Avery saw the same thing in the high school kids she tutored in the writing lab. Particularly the boys. She called their reactions the "Rahhh" principle. Fear, worry, disappointment, hurt—they all came out as Rahhh!!! Yes, she could see through Luke.

She tried not to analyze her children, but she knew something monumental—no, something cataclysmic—had happened not only to her but to them as well on the day their adored father died. Losing Paul was more than merely losing a husband and father. His absence created a shift in all their universes, placing each of them in new orbits. Wes had become the self-proclaimed head of the family. Jamie, her only daughter, constantly reverted to a newfound protective hovering mode. And Avery's previously lighthearted dreamer —Luke—had instantly catapulted out of latent adolescence and into a somber adulthood. The rapid shift in her youngest was the rudest awakening for Avery.

Her twenty-nine-year-old son-in-law, Brady, headed for the study. "I brought you a new set of ink cartridges. I'll go install them."

"Uh . . ." She stalled, but it was too late to create an adequate story to explain the disconnected pile of devices on the desk.

"Whoa." He offered an ominous chuckle as he closed the door and walked over to Avery a few moments later, eyebrows nearly reaching his receding hairline, as he carried the mangled remains of a USB cord, whose end had been ripped away. Avery hurried over to him, grabbed the wire, and smiled sheepishly as she shoved the contraption into the pocket of her apron.

Brady leaned close and whispered. "I don't think you gave the poor thing a fighting chance." Unlike Avery, he seemed unaffected by the questioning glare his wife was shooting him from across the room. "Want me to hook it all back up for you? I've got a spare USB cord out in my car."

Avery cringed with each whispered word. The more attention he focused on the problem, the wider her children's eyes grew. "That'd be just great," she muttered in a monotone as she hurried over to create some subterfuge by sautéing her Brussels sprouts.

The rest of the day progressed uneventfully. Wes stepped up and filled in for their absent patriarch, offering the blessing on the food. Everyone fell silent as that painful landmark was crossed. The meal, filled with family favorites, was accented with light banter—reminiscences of days past— though Avery noted the conspicuous way her children avoided mentioning Paul, as if their father was not only gone but had never existed at all. Feeling as if the best portion of her own life was being obliterated, she folded her napkin with a deliberateness that brought all conversation to a complete halt. When she looked up, she saw eight worried eyes riveted on her.

Jamie's nervous glance shifted to each of her brothers before she leaned over her plate and eyed Avery. "Are you all right, Mother?"

Avery noted how her daughter had recently begun referring to her as "Mother" instead of the previously expected "Mom." She disliked it immensely, but as she could barely speak, she responded with a rapid series of nods until she found her voice.

"It's all right to talk about your father," she finally managed to say. "Avoiding his memory doesn't ease my sorrow. In fact, ignoring his absence makes it more apparent."

"We just—uh—," mumbled Luke.

"I know, I know."

They slogged through dinner and the men cleared. Then, while she and Jamie did the dishes, Avery noticed the guys huddled near the TV. She didn't give it much thought other than to wince at the extravagance of her purchase.

The huddle broke up, and Brady suggested it was time to leave. Avery saw a new level of worry wash over Jamie about leaving her mother again.

Big brother Wes urged the old married couple to go as he wrapped Avery up in a hug, giving her an exaggerated shake. "Luke and I are going to school Mom in Mario Kart 101."

Avery laughed. "I don't think so, pal. The cook is ready to hit the hay."

"Mind if Luke and I stay and play?"

The question prompted Avery's mile-wide smile that seemed to give Jamie the comfort she needed to make a guilt-free exit. Avery gave the young marrieds a quick hug goodbye before turning back to her college singles. "All right, Mario and Luigi, I'm going to turn off all the downstairs lights except for the kitchen and family room."

Avery hit the study's light but the room still glowed from the repaired computer's monitor and the small desk lamp. Her gaze fell on the bookshelves where Paul's legal books and fifteen Avery Elkins Thompson first editions stood. Those novels were Paul's proudest possessions. Avery knew he had read each one at least three or four times, curled up in the big lounger by the bay window. They brought her no pleasure this night, nor had they any night since her muse died.

She sat at the computer. Just seeing its screen lit again felt wrong. There would be no sweet notes from Paul waiting in her email file, no links to exotic destinations to which they fantasized journeying. As she clicked the final command to shut down the computer, she noticed a little pile of USB connectors with a sticky note in Brady's handwriting. "Just in case," it read. Avery smiled. She adored that son-in-law of hers, though he and Jamie were a mismatched pair. Avery knew it was as much circumstance as passion that drew her perky, comely daughter to the scruffy TA, seven years her senior. Brady was a spiritual person, steady and kind, a marriageable version of the ailing father Jamie adored and had been steeling herself to lose for years. That fear and Paul's eventual loss had made her a tough and rigid woman at times, exerting control over her changing universe, and sweet Brady yielded to her as much as possible.

Avery sighed as she switched the desk lamp off and headed down the hall, passing the "wall of fame," where all the kids' photos were on display. She passed a favorite vacation photo and straightened it, though the frame already hung perfectly square. She knew the frame wasn't off. She was. More accurately, it was her reaction to a sweet moment from years ago on one of the family's nightly walks along the beach on Anna Maria Island in Florida that was off kilter. Jamie snapped the photo of Avery and Paul as they posed before the fabled beach house of a man who had become a legend along the island. Only after the photo was printed did Avery realize that Jamie had actually caught the widowed owner of the sprawling Victorian home standing like a solitary ghost on the widow's walk. He and his solemn, lonely watch contrasted sharply with the happy images of Avery and Paul in the foreground.

Avery's finger traced along the image of Gabriel Carson, the mysterious, romantic widower. He had so fascinated Avery's writer's instinct that she hounded the locals for more information on him until she discovered where his florist's shop was located. Her cheeks still flushed when she recalled how she studied the handsome loner from outside his business's storefront window, watching him chat and laugh with the waiting customers as he arranged their opulent bouquets. But when they exited, leaving him alone, Avery watched his eyes dim as his face settled into quiet soberness.

His aura had haunted her for weeks, and when she and the family returned home to Utah from their summer jaunt, she fashioned a character in one of her books after the intriguing Mr. Carson.

Avery bit her upper lip and shrank, as goosebumps spread across her arms in shame. How many times she had given thanks that she and Paul weren't that man, mired in enduring mourning. It all seemed so ironic. So selfish. So shameful.

"I'm right there with you," she said to the man in the photo.

ABOUT THE AUTHOR

Laurie (L.C.) Lewis will always be a Marylander at heart—a weather-whining lover of crabs, American history, and the sea. She admits to being craft-challenged, particularly lethal with a glue gun, and a devotee of sappy movies. Her ninth published novel, her first romance novella, *Sweet Water,* was inspired by a visit to Oregon's magnificent coastline, and Mother Eugenie, upon whom the character Mother Thomasine is based.

She is currently completing *Awakening Avery,* book three in her SECOND CHANCE ROMANCE SERIES. It's slated for a July 24th, 2018 release. Please enjoy the excerpt above.

Goodreads • Instagram • www.laurielclewis.com

ALSO BY LAURIE LEWIS

Laurie's women's fiction novels:

Love on a Limb

Sweet Water

The Dragons of Alsace Farm

Awakening Avery

Unspoken

Under the pen name L.C. Lewis, she
has written the award-winning
historical fiction series,
FREE MEN and DREAMERS,
set against the backdrop
of the War of 1812:

Dark Sky at Dawn (2007)

Twilight's Last Gleaming (2008)

Dawn's Early Light (2009)

Oh, Say Can You See? (2010)

In God is Our Trust (2011)

www.ingramcontent.com/pod-product-compliance
Lightning Source LLC
Chambersburg PA
CBHW071152260626
47162CB00003B/1024